Erin McEwan,
Your Days Are Numbered

Erin McEwan,
Your Days Are Numbered

by Alan Ritchie

Alfred A. Knopf ⟶ New York

THIS IS A BORZOI BOOK
PUBLISHED BY ALFRED A. KNOPF, INC.
Copyright © 1990 by Alan Ritchie
Jacket copyright © 1990 by Mark Buehner
All rights reserved under International and Pan-American Copyright
Conventions. Published in the United States by Alfred A. Knopf, Inc.,
New York, and simultaneously in Canada by Random House of Canada
Limited, Toronto. Distributed by Random House, Inc., New York.
Manufactured in the United States of America

2 4 6 8 0 9 7 5 3 1

Library of Congress Cataloging-in-Publication Data
Ritchie, Alan. Erin McEwan, your days are numbered /
Alan Ritchie.   p. cm.
Summary: If Erin doesn't start doing better in her
math class, she may have to repeat the whole year.
ISBN 0-679-80321-1 (trade)   ISBN 0-679-90321-6 (lib. bdg.)
[1. Schools—Fiction] I. Title.   PZ7.R5114Er   1989
[Fic]—dc19   89-2581

For Barbara

1

What Erin McEwan needed was a foghorn. Sitting right in her lap, preferably, so she could give it a loud toot and drown out her parents' voices. They had been arguing ever since they'd boarded the ferry for Halifax, bickering about every picky little thing in the world, from when to do the laundry to what to eat for dinner. They'd been arguing about everything except the one thing that mattered—the fact that Mrs. McEwan had lost her job.

But now, mercifully, there was a lull. Erin pointed to a low gray cloud a mile or two off the bow. "Fog's rolling in," she said. Weather, she thought, was a peaceful subject.

"Brrr," said Mrs. McEwan, wrapping her spring coat tightly around her. "It would be nice to work in Dartmouth, and not have to make this trip to Halifax every day. It's a blessing I lost that stupid job."

There. The unmentionable subject had finally been mentioned. Erin thought it might be safer to talk about the weather, but something was nagging her. "I *still* can't understand why you had to do math in your job, anyway," she said. "You're a cook. You're the best cook in Halifax."

"That's exactly what *I* said," said her mother.

"You even said you were the best cook in Halifax?" asked Mr. McEwan.

"I didn't *even* say it, I *especially* said it!" said Mrs. McEwan, her hair blowing in her face. She shrugged. "But all that foolish woman wanted to do was make a big deal about a bunch of numbers. What did she expect? She always knew I had problems with math."

Erin knew it too, and she was totally sympathetic. Math was a world of darkest confusion for Erin. She would rather be locked in a cupboard with a wild animal than forced to share her mind with a handful of numbers. Numbers performed strange unpredictable dances. They shrank. They grew unexpectedly. They vanished, or merged with others. And as they did so, her teacher and her father and most of the boys and girls in her sixth-grade class sang, "Math's easy! It's easy!" over and over until she could scream.

"You're going to be the big loser, I told her," said Mrs. McEwan. "There are dozens of places dying to get their hands on someone who cooks as well as I do. I'll get another job just like that." She snapped her fingers in the air.

"Sure you will," said Erin quickly.

Erin wished her father would say something too. But

4

he simply nodded his head vaguely. Finally he said, "Gosh, in all the excitement I completely forgot to tell you this horrible thing that happened to me and a bedpan yesterday morning."

Erin's father worked at a hospital, and he always had a good story to tell. Right now, Erin guessed, he just wanted to tell a story to distract her mother. And she was already giggling at his tale of woe. Erin had heard this particular story the previous evening before her mother arrived home with the dreadful news. It was long and funny and bound to last the rest of the way to Halifax.

She listened for a few moments, then stood up restlessly and began to pace the deck of the ferry. It was windier and colder on the opposite side, but the view was spectacular. Quite close to the ferry was a huge oil-drilling platform. Two large tugs were inching it down the harbor toward the open sea. The drilling platform itself, with its high-rise layers of crew housing and offices, was sitting more than a hundred feet above the water on top of gigantic cylindrical legs. In several days' time, when the rig reached its station on the Grand Banks of Newfoundland, the legs would be flooded with water. That would lower the rig to sit on the seafloor. Erin knew a lot about oil-drilling rigs because her father had once worked on them.

Erin had hardly known her father in those days. He was always away. As this thought passed through her mind she happened to glance along the rail of the ferry.

To her surprise there was her father, also leaning over the rail and staring out at the rig. Something about the look on her father's face drew her to him.

Mr. McEwan had an intense stare that made him look either startled or angry. In fact he only very occasionally lost his temper. Now, as she moved to the rail beside him, Erin could feel sparks of annoyance crackling from his shoulders.

"Hi," he said in a strangled voice.

"Where's Mom?"

"She got cold and went down below."

"What? Not in the middle of one of your stories?" That surprised Erin and worried her slightly. Perhaps her mother wasn't handling things quite as well as she seemed to be.

"I must be losing my touch," said Mr. McEwan. Erin knew that statement was supposed to be a joke, but his voice was full of anger.

"You're not mad at Mom, are you?" said Erin cautiously.

"What?" said Mr. McEwan. "Why?"

"For losing her job? For not being good at math?"

"Oh, no, no. Of course not. Your mother does the best she can. I'm just angry at—at— I don't know, things. Everything."

They were both silent for a few moments.

Then Mr. McEwan said, "Angry at myself, really." He jerked his chin out at the drilling platform. "A friend of mine called the other day. Asked if I wanted a maintenance job on that very rig. I should have said yes."

Erin turned to him, horrified. "Dad! Surely you're not giving up now?" she said.

Her father had done nothing connected with the oil business for more than three years. A drop in the price of oil had put him out of work. For a while Erin's family had been sorely pinched.

"I'm getting out," her father had finally said. He had looked around and chosen a profession in which there were more jobs than people to fill them. He waited until finally, at long last, Erin's mother landed a good job. Then, to the complete astonishment of his family, to say nothing of his flabbergasted steelworking, shipbuilding, and oil-rigging friends, he began three years of training to be a nurse. He was heading into his last year now, and the family had scrimped and sacrificed to get him this far.

"Well, you're *not* giving up, are you?" Erin repeated her question.

Erin's father didn't respond for a long time. He continued to stare at the oil rig.

Finally he said, "I guess not, no."

"Are you sure?" said Erin.

His voice grew firmer, and he reached out and put his arm around his daughter. "No, don't worry. Of course I'm not giving up."

Erin allowed herself a small sigh of relief. She couldn't

really imagine what might make him change his mind anyway. He hadn't missed oil rigs. Indeed, he was delighted, enthralled with his new profession. He had spent many evenings entertaining Erin and her mother with funny stories about the trials of a middle-aged oil rigger trying to keep up with trainee nurses fifteen years his junior.

"It's not a question of giving up. I may not have any choice," said her father after a moment, upsetting Erin's peace of mind.

"But Mom *will* get another job," said Erin. "She's a great cook. Everybody knows that!"

"Erin," said her father gently. "You have to understand it's not a question of how good a cook your mother is. The question is, Are there any jobs for cooks, good *or* bad? And the answer, I'm afraid, is very few, maybe none. That's the problem."

"Honest?" said Erin, seriously troubled now. She knew that jobs were hard to find in Halifax, indeed in all the Maritime Provinces. And yet somehow she had not connected that fact to her mother.

"And I've still got another year of school before I can start earning any money as a nurse," he said.

"Could we borrow some money?" said Erin. "If we had to, I mean."

Her father sighed. "We're already up to our ears with loans, Erin. There's the mortgage on the house, and my student loan, and—well, look, if we want to keep the house, it all boils down to your mother finding a new job pretty quickly. Otherwise . . ." He didn't finish his sentence but looked out at the oil rig again.

Her father's ominous words made Erin certain that she was about to do the right thing. She didn't understand why everyone else was giving up so quickly on her mother's old job. Erin certainly wasn't. Her parents might think she was coming over to Halifax to keep them company, but Erin had other plans. Now that they were sailing the last few hundred yards toward the Halifax Ferry Terminal, Erin could see her own private destination quite clearly just off to the left along the waterfront. It was a collection of renovated docks and warehouses known as the Historic Properties. If everything went well, Erin would be there in just a few minutes, finding out what had *really* happened to her mother's job. But first she had to ditch her parents.

It turned out to be easy. When she and her father went downstairs into the ferry, they were separated from Mrs. McEwan by the crush of passengers shuffling toward the exit. Erin grabbed her father's hand and lifted it up to wave across the crowd to her mother. That let her mother know Erin planned to accompany her father, who was making a quick trip to fetch some textbooks at the Halifax Infirmary Hospital, where he was training.

Her mother was on her way to pick up a dress she had already paid for and now wished she hadn't bought. Mrs. McEwan gave Erin and her father a parting wave, then marched rapidly ahead of them into the streets of

Halifax. Following some distance behind, the pair watched her turn off down a side street. At that moment Erin stopped.

"I've changed my mind," she said to her father. "I'm going to go and shop with Mom instead." She gave him a quick kiss on the cheek, then ran after her mother. She didn't catch her, though. As soon as Erin was out of her father's sight, she slowed down to a crawl until the short, red-headed figure of her mother disappeared around another corner up ahead.

It was as easy as that. Alone, Erin changed direction and set off toward the Historic Properties, barely two blocks away.

2

The Historic Properties was part of a waterfront renewal plan, and in summer it was an important tourist attraction, filled with strolling people. Here was a dock for the *Bluenose II*, a replica of the fishing schooner that had once been the pride of Atlantic Canada—the schooner that was engraved on the back of the Canadian ten-cent piece. As she walked along the cobblestones, she could see the masts of the *Bluenose II* rising above the old stone buildings. Today nobody strolled between the buildings, not with that bitter wind blowing off the water.

Two thirds of the way along a low stone warehouse she turned to her right. An old-fashioned hanging sign picked out in curlicues read SBROCCHI. This was the place. She took a deep breath and opened the door. A cheery bell jingled in the back.

The shop was empty, as it often was in late afternoon. Except in tourist season, of course, when it was busy all the time.

"Sbrocchi's" was a mistake that worked, the owner

11

had once explained cheerfully to Erin. The shop had opened one spring several years previously as Sbrocchi's Nova Scotia Cookcraft.

"Sbrocchi? Now that's a fine old Nova Scotia name," Erin's father had remarked, long before her mother had gone to work there. Nova Scotia had been settled first by French and then by Scots. Sbrocchi sounded, if anything, Italian.

Italian it was. And if Sbrocchi wasn't a fine old Nova Scotia name, the tourists were happy to make it a fine new one. The first summer was a great success. Maple syrup, jams, jellies, pies, cookbooks, including *Bluenose Cookery*, were piled even now in great stacks by the far door. Through the glass of the opposite door Erin could see the huge bowsprit of the *Bluenose* schooner.

Business had boomed until September. Suddenly, bang, the door swung shut and didn't open again. The shop stayed empty. The tourists were gone.

Halifax residents stopped by for the odd jar of jam, but by October of that year it was clear that Sbrocchi Nova Scotia Cookcraft would have to change its spots or sink into Halifax harbor before spring.

Now, six years later, it had changed. The name was shorter, and the store was only partly a Nova Scotia cookcraft store. During much of the year it prospered as a gourmet grocery store. And it did a roaring business at lunchtime all year long as a takeout delicatessen, specializing in particularly scrumptious pasta dishes. There was a stretch in late afternoon that was getting busier every day as office workers stopped to take out a quick and tasty dinner.

Erin slipped quietly into the store, looking for the owner. She wasn't in the Nova Scotia cookcraft aisle, nor the cookbook aisle. She wasn't along the back, where there was a general hodgepodge of gourmet items and three large freezers. Nor was she in the delicatessen aisle, with its different kinds of bread and its split personality, one that couldn't make up its mind whether it was Jewish or German or Italian.

Erin circled back to the large takeout counter at the front of the shop that was the heart and soul of the Sbrocchi success. Behind it was someone Erin had never seen before. At first Erin was taken aback. Then she realized she shouldn't be surprised. After all, her mother was gone and somebody had to take her place, even temporarily. Erin studied the woman for a moment. She was thin and elegant, with graying hair. Her dress, under a shop apron, looked expensive.

How had Mrs. Sbrocchi managed to find somebody so fast? Then a nasty thought struck her. Mrs. Sbrocchi must have *planned* to fire her mother. How else could she have somebody ready to take her mother's place? Erin's hopes shrank. Had she wasted her time making this trip? She hesitated and was actually turning back toward the door when the lady behind the counter looked up and noticed her.

And what the woman did then made Erin's heart fall even further.

Her mother, Erin knew, would have called out a cheerful question while continuing to work away behind the counter. Mrs. McEwan generally directed customers with hand waves, like a workman guiding a dump truck. "Back, back, now down, down, up a bit, that's it!" until they found what they were looking for on the shelves. That kind of thing.

But this new woman? She was far too elegant to do that. Instead she swept gracefully out from behind the counter, and to Erin's astonishment actually seized her hand and shook it.

"Well, hello," she said. "I'm Sally Eberhardt. I couldn't help but notice you looked a little lost." She smiled warmly. "I'm afraid I'm a little lost myself. I've only started working here today. But I'm positive that between us we can find what you're looking for."

Goodness, Mrs. Eberhardt was so pleasant and gracious that she made Erin feel like a princess arriving at a ball. She now knew for certain that she was wasting her time. How could her mother get her job back from this person? It would be like competing with the Queen.

But she'd come this far, so she said, "Is Mrs. Sbrocchi here, please?"

"Why, yes, she's in the office," said Mrs. Eberhardt with another warm smile. "But I'm afraid she's busy at the moment."

And I'm just a little girl, thought Erin, not meant to interrupt important grownups. Erin decided she didn't like this smooth and silken creature after all. What right did she have to prevent her from seeing Mrs. Sbrocchi?

"It's personal," said Erin. "And important."

"Well, I'm afraid—" the woman began. But Erin really didn't need help anyway. She knew where the office was. She turned and walked swiftly down the aisle to the back, ignoring the politely firm "Excuse me!" that followed her. She knocked on a decorated oak door, opened it, and poked her head into the room.

"Mrs. Sbrocchi?" she said.

At the back of a crowded, cluttered room sat a short, chubby lady with auburn hair and heavy lipstick. She was wearing one of her usual gray suits that looked as if it would hold up for only a few moments longer before it burst, causing Mrs. Sbrocchi to flow out heaven only knew how far in every direction. Mrs. Sbrocchi half-turned from her desk, which was littered with papers and jars of jelly, and pulled her glasses down to the end of her nose.

"Erin!" she said, with her faint Italian accent. She rose quickly and bustled across the room to warmly embrace Erin, who was a full half-head taller.

"How are you, how are you?" said Mrs. Sbrocchi. "Not very good, I guess, after the bad news." And she held Erin away from her with both hands and looked up into her face. Mrs. Sbrocchi sniffed loudly, and Erin could see real tears welling up in her eyes.

"There!" said Mrs. Sbrocchi. "You're the one who should be crying, and here *I* am." She swiped at the tear and knocked the glasses off her nose. Then she and

Erin both bent together to pick them up and bumped heads. They both laughed. "See, I never change," said Mrs. Sbrocchi. "I'm a mess."

"No, no, you're not," said Erin, even though she was. Her mother was something of the same kind of mess. Which was why, Erin had always felt, the two women got on so well.

"What happened?" she asked.

Mrs. Sbrocchi didn't seem to think it was an unreasonable question, but she did look guilty. "Come," she said, "come," and began to draw Erin by the arm into the room.

"Sit! Sit," she said. "No, not in my chair, I'm the old lady."

"No, you're not, Mrs. Sbrocchi," said Erin. Mrs. Sbrocchi laughed and shoveled some of the debris further back on the desk so Erin could hoist herself up onto the corner. Then she looked at Erin for a moment and shook her head.

"Erin, what could I do?" she said.

"I don't know," said Erin. "I didn't even know anything was wrong."

"Yes, you did," said Mrs. Sbrocchi. "You didn't come here by accident nearly every day to help your mother clean up."

"It was nothing," protested Erin. "It was just—"

"It was just if *you* didn't come and help, your mother often didn't get home till eight, did she? Sometimes even later?"

"True," admitted Erin.

"Well, now I'll tell you something else," said Mrs. Sbrocchi. "If I hadn't come in to help out every afternoon, your mother might never have left here at all."

"But this is your store," said Erin. "You *had* to be here."

"Erin, this store was meant to be a part-time job for me, not full-time. When I made your mother an assistant manager, she was supposed to take on extra responsibilities. She couldn't, and that's that."

"But I've heard you say she could cook like an Italian!"

"I said that?" said Mrs. Sbrocchi. "Well, perhaps I did."

"Wasn't that good enough?"

"It was always good enough, Erin. For that, she didn't need a promotion. No, I needed help doing the books, ordering stock, pricing things."

"I thought she was trying to help."

"Erin, Erin. Sooner or later you have to stop *trying* to help, you have to actually help. She couldn't even add up the cash. No—that's not true. She could add up the cash, over and over, with a different answer every time. That's how bad it was."

"Oh," said Erin, digesting this information and feeling uneasy. She wasn't particularly good with long columns of numbers herself.

"Couldn't you have given her more time?" she said after a moment.

"Time?" said Mrs. Sbrocchi. "I've got nothing but time. I've got so much time I'm sitting here all afternoon gabbing with you. Here, help me put on these labels." She slipped off the desk and began to write prices on a string of labels. Erin began to stick them on some jelly jars, and for a moment they worked together in silence. Then there was a discreet knock at the door. Mrs. Eberhardt's head appeared.

"I'm sorry to interrupt, but there's a lady out here asking for you," she said.

"Oh. Ah," said Mrs. Sbrocchi, looking frazzled. "Can you tell her I'm busy?"

"I think you'd better come," said Mrs. Eberhardt. "She seems very upset."

Erin trailed Mrs. Sbrocchi as she left the office. The lady was indeed *very* upset. She was pacing back and forth at the front of the shop, clutching a jar of something.

When Mrs. Sbrocchi approached, the woman thrust out the jar as if dealing a death blow with a sword. "You sold me this!" she said angrily.

"Why, yes, quite probably," said Mrs. Sbrocchi, taking the jar and examining it. "What seems to be—oh!" She had turned it over to read the price label on the jar.

"Oh? 'Oh' is not what I said, I can tell you, when I found a jar of it in Saint John, New Brunswick, for three seventy-five," said the angry woman. "Nine dollars and seventy-five cents you charged me."

"How terrible," said Mrs. Sbrocchi soothingly. "Somehow the wrong price sticker has stuck to the jar. We'd never charge you that much on purpose."

"You wouldn't?" said the woman, stamping up the Nova Scotia cookcraft aisle.

"Look at the others!" said the woman. And sure enough, the same $9.75 price was marked on each label. "I buy this brand all the time," she said. "I never even bother to look at the price."

Erin had eased her way down the aisle, following the argument, and now could see the labels clearly herself. What disturbed her was that the neat hand-printing on each label was her mother's.

"I can assure you that we mark things up by fifty percent at the most," said Mrs. Sbrocchi. "I'm afraid there must have been an error on the invoice that came to us with the shipment."

"Well, there wasn't," said the woman firmly. "Because it was at your supplier's in Saint John where I bought my other jar. She found her copy of your invoice. There was no error on it. She is very upset too. She had to come to Halifax today, and she said she'd meet me here."

"Oh. Oh dear." Mrs. Sbrocchi looked flustered and trapped. Erin was beginning to wish that she was somewhere else. Then Mrs. Eberhardt spoke.

"Please come and sit down, Mrs. . . ?" she said, taking the other woman by the arm.

"Aikman," said the woman grudgingly.

"Dear Mrs. Aikman," said Mrs. Eberhardt as she smoothly guided the woman back toward the office. "I know this is no excuse, but we've been having terrible trouble just recently with one of our staff. I'm afraid we've had to let her go, and I think you'll find—"

She broke off as Mrs. Sbrocchi caught up with her and went up on tiptoe to whisper in Mrs. Eberhardt's ear. But Mrs. Sbrocchi wasn't very good at whispering, and everyone heard her say, "That's her daughter."

Erin wanted to sink through the floor.

Both Mrs. Aikman and Mrs. Eberhardt looked back toward Erin with knowing eyes. Then the two woman moved on silently into the office.

"Erin, I'm so sorry," said Mrs. Sbrocchi, "but could you come back later? Perhaps tomorrow. Only as you can see—"

Erin nodded quickly, and started to walk toward the door. Her mouth was quivering. Mrs. Sbrocchi followed her.

"I'm sorry too, Mrs. Sbrocchi," said Erin as she paused by the door. "I didn't realize your problems were that bad. I guess I understand now why you fired her."

"Fired her?" said Mrs. Sbrocchi, astonished. "No, no, no!"

"No?" said Erin, confused.

"Of course not. Your mother quit."

Erin was stunned. "Quit? But why?"

Mrs. Sbrocchi looked distressed. "Of course I still

wanted her to stay on and cook. But as assistant manager? Impossible. What could I do, Erin? I offered to give her the same job as before. She was insulted. She's crazy."

But this was wonderful news! "Don't worry, Mrs. Sbrocchi," said Erin eagerly. "In a day or so I'm sure she'll want to work for you again."

Mrs. Sbrocchi shook her head sadly. "It's not possible, Erin. Things went too far. Things were said. I called your mother Mrs. McPighead."

"I'm sure she'll forgive you," said Erin McPighead, thinking there were times when it was a pretty good name for her mother.

"But I won't forgive her. She called me, well, lots of names," said Mrs. Sbrocchi. "She called me fat!"

Erin glanced down at Mrs. Sbrocchi stout body and said nothing. There was a moment of silence. Then they both laughed.

"It's not funny," said Mrs. Sbrocchi crossly, when she had finally wiped the smile off her own face. "We were friends, yes. But there are things you just don't say to people, friends or not." She waved her arms around her. "And now look. To leave me suddenly with all the cooking. I was trying to do less work. Now I'm stuck doing more. I can't forgive that, either."

She narrowed her eyes and looked closely at Erin for a moment. "Hey, you know a little about how things work around here, don't you?"

Erin nodded.

"You wouldn't like a job after school for a few hours every day?"

Erin opened and closed her mouth, speechless with surprise.

"Me?" she said at last.

"Yes, you!" Mrs. Sbrocchi, grasped Erin's hands. "You're just the person I need."

"But—"

"We're busy, busy, busy, and everything's a mess! Even though you're young, you're a hard worker."

"Really, Mrs. Sbrocchi, I don't—"

"I have to go, but you think about it, Erin," said Mrs. Sbrocchi. She lowered her voice to a whisper and said, "Mrs. Eberhardt is so nice, and she's so smart, but she can't cook and she's *so* slow, and oh, Erin, I need someone who knows where everything goes. Promise you'll call me?"

"I, er— Okay," said Erin, feeling guilty because she was actually talking about a job with the very person who had fired her mother. At the same time she felt pleased that somebody thought she was good at something.

3

Erin was sitting in a chair beside the desk of her home-room teacher, feeling uncomfortable and staring at the marble pattern on the green floor tiles. The room smelled faintly of school disinfectant, the green sawdust kind. The whole new wing of the school had that same un-interesting smell. So far Erin hadn't much liked her three years in the new wing. She found it dull, from its pink brick outside to its cream-colored classrooms with their muddy green floors. But now, at the end of her last year in Queen Anne School, she was beginning to have sec-ond thoughts.

Would Dartmouth Junior High be any better? It might easily be worse. Queen Anne floor tiles might not be interesting, but they were familiar and comforting.

The conversation suddenly shifted away from the un-usually cool weather and onto the subject of Erin her-self. "In general, I must say I've been very pleased with Erin's schoolwork over the past year," said Mr. Wall. Erin looked up and flashed a grateful smile at her homeroom teacher, who looked uncomfortable. But then, he always did. He was a small man with wire-rim glasses. His suits always seemed a little too large for him, and Erin always wished that he'd sit up a little straighter. He looked as if one day he'd accidentally slip right down through his shirt and all of him would end up in his trousers. Erin liked him a lot.

Sitting beside Erin were her mother and father. They looked uncomfortable too, but the news that Erin was generally doing well caused a slight smile to appear on her mother's lips. She glanced at Erin fondly.

"Except—" said Mr. Wall. The smile on Mrs. McEwan's face faded. And here it was: the great big "except."

Erin stared out the streaky window of her classroom. Across the courtyard she could see the old wing of Queen Anne School. It was a low building covered with white asphalt shingles. Inside, the old wood floors creaked horribly and the air smelled of poster paint and overripe apples. Erin wished she was back in the old wing now. It housed kindergarten to grade three. Over there, math was pretty easy.

"The problem, I'm afraid, is mathematics," said Mr. Wall.

I knew it, thought Erin. She stopped listening. Erin had heard it all before, mostly from Mr. Murdoch, her math teacher, whom she didn't like very much.

She thought instead about Mrs. Sbrocchi. Erin had promised to call on Saturday. It was now the following

Wednesday, and Erin had done nothing. For the last three days she had been hoping against hope that her mother would come bouncing home to announce she had patched up her quarrel with Mrs. Sbrocchi or had somehow found a new job. Neither of those miracles had happened. So here they all were, the entire out-of-work McEwan family, all available for a school interview.

What should I do? wondered Erin. Could it possibly help my mother's chances of getting her job back if I work for Mrs. Sbrocchi?

Suddenly Mr. Wall's words jerked Erin's attention back to the interview. "Mr. Murdoch, Erin's math teacher, feels that unless something is done quickly to improve Erin's math skills, it might be advisable to hold Erin back for a year," he said.

What? Fail me? thought Erin, horrified. It was one thing to want to stay in dear old Queen Anne School, but quite another when all your friends went on to Dartmouth Junior High and left you behind! She jerked her head around and faced Mr. Wall with such a fierce stare that he shrank down even further into his suit. Mr. McEwan took one look at the expression on his daughter's face and kicked her sharply on the ankle.

The McEwan family arrived home in a straggling line, cheeriest at the front, gloomiest at the back.

First was Mrs. McEwan. Her spirits were high. She had dismissed this latest bad news so quickly it made

Erin nervous. "There's really no point in worrying, dear," she had said with a shrug. "Some of us will never be any good at math. There's nothing at all we can do about it." The advice was intended to be comforting, but it didn't make Erin feel much better. Is she trying to convince me or herself? Erin wondered.

Mrs. McEwan went straight in the door, heading for the kitchen, where she had been proving dinner by dinner for the last five nights that she was a truly great cook, even on a tight budget.

Next to arrive in front of the house was Erin. Erin had kept herself from becoming completely miserable by saying to herself over and over, "It's just a warning. Everybody gets warnings. It doesn't mean they'll actually fail me." She had almost managed to convince herself.

Erin dawdled at the rusty front gate, waiting for her father. She looked up at their narrow two-story clapboard house and wondered, Was it really possible that they would lose it? It was the last in a row of similar houses, the most dilapidated of all. If you looked closely, you could see a faint sag in the end wall. Inside, that sagging made all the stairs up to the bedrooms dip to one side. Her father had said it would be an expensive job to fix the stairs. Erin didn't mind them the way they were. Anyway, they were a long way down on the list of great plans the McEwans had for fixing up their house.

The trouble was, they had bought the house barely two months before Mr. McEwan lost his oil-rig job, and it had been all the family could do to pay the mortgage, let alone make renovations.

Erin loved the house, but it was still painted a color that made her ill. It had been a horrible shade of maroon when they first moved in and it was still maroon, faded and peeling and growing uglier day by day. Just inside the front door, however, were three gallons of a lovely slate blue paint that had been waiting for spring and a little spare time in Mr. McEwan's schedule.

As the gloomiest McEwan of all finally caught up with her, Erin wondered whether there ever *would* be any spare time for her father. Erin's school interview had for some reason hit him hardest. Mr. McEwan himself was struggling with the classwork part of his training. He had exams coming up, and was spending long hours studying. In spite of this he had made arrangements to work extra shifts as a nursing assistant whenever possible in order to make a little more money for the family. Mr. McEwan, looking exhausted, managed a small smile and shooed Erin ahead of him into the house.

"How is it?" said Mrs. McEwan anxiously, bringing her own plate to the table and sitting down.

"As if you didn't know!" said Erin, with a full mouth.

"She's fishing for compliments again," said Mr. McEwan. The macaroni and cheese was too hot for him, and he was blowing gently on it.

"I *never* fish for compliments," said Mrs. McEwan indignantly, digging into her own plateful. "At least, I never used to before. People used to *automatically* make compliments." She gave a heavy, theatrical sigh. "Well, I guess my cooking just isn't what it used—" Erin and her father drowned out Mrs. McEwan's speech with a chorus of mock groans.

As usual, the macaroni and cheese was a triumph. Totally unlike the bland stuff that came out of a box, their evening meal was cleverly spiced, made with two different kinds of cheese. Delicious chunks of leftover ham lurked everywhere in the sauce. On top there was a scrumptious, buttery crust made with homemade breadcrumbs. When Erin's mother was cooking, even the most inexpensive meal was delicious. For a while the kitchen fell silent as the McEwans drowned their sorrows in hot cheese.

The kitchen was the action center of the McEwan household and the only room that had so far received any renovation money. The walls had been re-covered in a bright floral paper, and all the cupboards were painted a matching canary yellow. But the countertops were old and stained, and the previous owner's dog, shut regularly in the kitchen, had ripped half the linoleum off the floor in anger, revealing wide gray boards beneath.

Every Christmas for three years Mr. McEwan had promised a big new stove, and every Christmas he had been not quite able to afford it. Most of their meals were eaten at the kitchen table that had been left behind in the house. It was a dreadful thing, with rusting chrome legs. It was covered with a pattern of little white ducks waddling between old cigarette burns.

But in spite of its shortcomings, the kitchen was bright and cheerful. Most important of all, it was home to the best cook in Dartmouth, in Halifax County, probably in Nova Scotia, if it came to that. Dessert was Mrs. McEwan's famous blueberry pie. It was Erin's favorite dessert. "You're a *perfect* cook," said Erin as she finished off her second piece of pie.

Her mother beamed. She stood up and went over to the fridge. From the top she pulled a fistful of newspaper clippings and shook them in the air.

"These are all people looking for cooks."

"*That* many?" exclaimed Erin, delighted.

"Don't you worry," continued Mrs. McEwan. "One of them at least will realize that I *am* perfect."

"If you were really perfect, you'd be modest, too," said Erin with a laugh.

"All I ever get is an argument," said Mrs. McEwan in mock annoyance. "All right, all right, just a perfect *cook*, then."

Erin glanced at her father and was disappointed to see that he wasn't enjoying the family banter. She caught his eye and received a weak smile.

Then, once again, he changed the subject. "I'm sorry I kicked your ankle this afternoon, Erin," said her father. "I know it was a shock. It was a shock to all of us."

Erin nodded.

"If you'd stared at Mr. Wall like that for a moment longer, he would have melted into a blob."

"Serve him right. Horrible little man," said Mrs. McEwan.

"Actually he's very nice," interjected Erin.

" 'Of course, Mrs. McEwan, *you* realize just how important math skills are,' " said Erin's mother, mimicking Mr. Wall. "I'll bet he heard I lost my job because I can't do math either and said that just to rub it in."

"Tch. That's silly," said Mr. McEwan.

Mrs. McEwan supposed it was silly. "If he'd known about it he'd hardly have suggested we hire a private tutor," she said.

There was an awkward silence. Everyone knew there was no money available for private tutors. There was money for macaroni and cheese, and not a lot more.

Then the phone rang. It was a welcome interruption, and Erin's mother went into the living room to answer it. She came back and looked at Erin oddly. "It's for you," she said.

"I thought you were going to call me," said Mrs. Sbrocchi accusingly when Erin picked up the phone.

"I was. Only—"

"Can you do it? Just for a few weeks," pleaded Mrs. Sbrocchi. "Please! Just until Mrs. Eberhardt learns the ropes. You'll save my life."

"Mrs. Sbrocchi, I can't—" began Erin.

"Look, I know you're too young to work, according

30

to the law. But I know what you can do, and it's worth good money," said Mrs. Sbrocchi.

"But I—"

"I'm sure your family is going to need it."

This stopped Erin for a moment. Her family indeed might need the money. After a pause, she took a breath and said, "I—"

"Just three hours, say from four to seven during the week. And maybe on Saturday."

"Mrs. Sbrocchi, are you going to let me get a word in edgewise?" said Erin.

"Sure, sure, Erin. Of course."

"Mrs. Sbrocchi, I just found out that I'm going to fail my grade at school if I don't get any better at math. I've got to spend all my spare time until the end of June studying."

"Oh," she said. "Oh dear." There was a long pause.

"They want me to take private tutoring," said Erin, trying hard to keep the quaver out of her voice.

"Good idea," said Mrs. Sbrocchi.

"But of course we can't afford it now."

"Ah. Yes," said Mrs. Sbrocchi, sounding a little guilty. There was another long silence.

"You know what?" said Mrs. Sbrocchi.

"What?"

"I've got *just* the answer. You come and help me, and I'll help you."

"How?"

"With math, Erin. There's lots of math to do in a store. We'll have you on the right track in no time!"

When Erin sat back down at the dinner table, she tried to avoid her mother's stare.

"I didn't know any of your friends had an Italian accent," said Mrs. McEwan.

"Oh yes. One or two of them," said Erin vaguely.

"Like who?"

"Oh, er—"

"That wasn't a call from the store, was it?"

Erin took a deep breath and prepared to jump into hot water. "If you mean Mrs. Sbrocchi, yes, it was her," said Erin.

"What did *she* want?" said Erin's mother angrily.

"Well," said Erin hesitantly. "Well, actually . . ." Then she made up her mind and spit it out in a rush. "She called to offer me a job."

"Oh!" said Mrs. McEwan, her face draining white. "Oh!" she said again, breathlessly, as if someone had punched her in the stomach. She sat silently for a moment with her mouth quivering. And then, to the absolute horror of Erin and her father, Mrs. McEwan burst into tears and fled from the room.

Erin and Mr. McEwan looked at each other helplessly. Neither of them could remember the last time Erin's mother had cried.

After a very long moment, they both got up and followed her into the living room. Mrs. McEwan was leaning into a corner of the room and sobbing. Mr. McEwan went up to her and put his arms around her. Erin, who was now actually a little taller than both her parents, came up behind her father and put her arms around as many bits of both of them as she could reach. For a long while they all stood like that, while Mrs. McEwan's sobs slowly died. In the end Erin was sniffling herself. It was turning out to be one of the rottenest days in her life. Everyone was out of work except her, it seemed. And she couldn't take the job because she was just about to fail her grade. She wished she was on the inside of the little group being hugged, instead of on the outside doing the hugging.

After about fifteen minutes they led the puffy-eyed Mrs. McEwan back to finish the cold macaroni. Erin's mother had stopped crying, and now she was being terribly reasonable. Both Erin and her father found this just as upsetting as tears because it was so unusual.

"I know it's not your fault, Erin," said her mother. "I can't blame you because you're a good worker. But I can't help feeling that she's offering you the job just to spite me."

"I'm sure she's not," said Mr. McEwan.

"Yes, yes, you're probably right," said Erin's mother.

"I won't do the work if it upsets you, Mom," said Erin.

"Wait a minute, wait a minute," said Mr. McEwan.

"We're all missing the point here. Will Erin actually have any time for after-school jobs? What about math homework?"

"Yes," said Erin. It was just the point she had made to Mrs. Sbrocchi. Should she mention the store owner's offer? "Mrs. Sbrocchi actually said she'd help me with my math."

"Well, you don't have to go all the way to Halifax for that," said Mr. McEwan. He reached over and squeezed Erin's hand. "I'll help you all I can."

"Couldn't we use the money?" said Erin.

But now it was her mother's turn to reach over and grasp Erin's hand, her eyes watering.

"Oh, Erin," she said. "It's sweet of you to worry about that and want to help. But don't you worry; I'm too good a cook to be out of a job for long. You'll see. It's nothing that your father and I want you to worry about. Promise."

Erin leaned over and kissed her mother on the cheek, and promised not to worry. But she knew that it was going to be a very difficult promise to keep.

"So it's settled then?" said Mr. McEwan.

"Yes," said Erin. She would spend every single afternoon, not working at Sbrocchi, but doing math. Now that she had made up her mind she felt a lot better.

For a little while there was an uneasy togetherness in the house. Everyone sat together on the couch in the living room and watched TV. Then gradually a sickness began to grow in the pit of Erin's stomach. She could see herself sitting, hour after hour, staring at her math books, doing her homework over and over again. The trouble was, she'd already tried staring at problems for ages. But when you just didn't know, you just didn't know. Extra hours of study didn't help. Her father meant well with his offer to help. But he was spending long hours at the hospital. Taking away that, and his homework time, and a few hours of sleep, there wasn't much time left to help Erin.

So for all this homework she was planning to do, would she actually be learning anything? If not, she'd be just as well off helping Mrs. Sbrocchi and earning some money.

It was a quarter to midnight when Erin quietly pulled the phone into the kitchen, closed the door, and dialed.

"Hello?"

"Is that you, Mrs. Sbrocchi?"

"Erin? Speak up. Is that you, Erin? Do you know what time it is?"

"I don't want to wake my parents," said Erin, still whispering. "Listen, I'm really sorry, Mrs. Sbrocchi. I talked to my parents, and they won't let me take the job."

"Oh," said Mrs. Sbrocchi. "Oh dear."

"I'm sorry," said Erin again.

Mrs. Sbrocchi sighed and said, "I am too, Erin." And indeed she sounded sorry. "After I talked to you, I began to wonder whether perhaps Mrs. McPighead's

35

daughter couldn't show her mother that a little simple math in a store isn't impossible to learn, and after that perhaps . . ." She paused.

"What are you saying, Mrs. Sbrocchi?" said Erin.

"Nothing, only . . . nothing. I'm sure your parents are quite right. Now you get going on your homework, Erin, and don't worry about me. I'll manage."

After Erin had hung up she was certain Mrs. Sbrocchi had hinted that her mother might go back to the store. What was needed was for Erin to show her mother that math wasn't all that hard. Ha! What an unlikely thing that was!

And anyway, what about all those cooking jobs that were available? They were still in a neat pile on top of the fridge. Curious, Erin pulled them down and began to glance through them. Then she frowned and looked again more closely. After a moment she sat down at the table and began to divide the clippings into piles.

When she was finished, she was depressed. Now she knew why her father had not been particularly cheerful at the sight of the stack of clippings.

Four of the clippings described the same job. They had been cut out from the morning *Halifax Chronicle-Herald* every day for four days. Four more described the exact same job advertised for the same four days in the evening paper—the *Halifax Mail-Star*. There were two clippings for a job in Bedford, which was too far away for a family without a car. And there was one clipping from the Saint John, New Brunswick, paper for a job in Saint John, which was clear across Nova Scotia and the Bay of Fundy, a hundred miles away. That one was just plain ridiculous!

Carefully Erin put the stack of clippings back on the fridge. Who does Mom think she's kidding? she wondered. And once again she found herself thinking about Mrs. Sbrocchi's proposal. If there really weren't many new jobs around, then suppose she *could* help get her mother's old job back? It might be the only way her father could finish his training.

Would it be worth losing a year of school? Possibly.

Would it be worth directly disobeying her parents? She could not remember having done that before, not on anything so important.

However. Nobody had said in so many words that she could *not* work in the store. Her parents had left it up to her, and Erin hadn't even voiced her decision out loud. She had decided herself not to take the job. Could she un-decide it? In spite of what her mother had said about not worrying, Erin knew that the money problem was very serious. Even a little bit from Erin might help.

If she took the job and nobody knew about it, there couldn't be a fuss, could there? But really, how could she possibly take a job clear across the harbor for three hours every afternoon and hide the fact from her parents? That was impossible.

Or was it? Everything was so confusing that once she was in bed, she lay awake for a long time staring at the discolored blotch on the ceiling. The blotch had been caused by a leaky roof a year ago. Her father had mended the roof, and Erin had promised to paint the blotch. The trouble was, she enjoyed staring at it. It helped her solve late-night problems. By the time she fell asleep, though, she had made up her mind about only one thing. She rolled over at last, after making a faithful promise to herself, and to her father. It was time to paint over the blotch.

4

Mr. Murdoch, Erin's math teacher, was horribly torturing a third-grade boy. The poor little kid had made the mistake of shouting down the hall right outside Mr. Murdoch's open door. Mr. Murdoch wasn't actually *doing* anything. He didn't have to. His fearsome reputation did all the torturing for him. Mr. Murdoch just sat, staring, while the poor kid stood in front of him and shook like a leaf. Mr. Murdoch was a tall, thin man, with a sharp hooked nose, thin lips, and pale blue, unblinking eyes. When he hunched down over his desk he was a vulture, and the kids he was staring at knew they were dead meat. Everyone in the school between kindergarten and fifth grade was scared to death of Mr. Murdoch.

But not sixth-grade kids. Behind the unfortunate boy Erin's sixth-grade math class was hugging itself with delight. Everyone except Erin, that is. She did not find Mr. Murdoch's torture sessions amusing.

"It was *you* I heard shouting, wasn't it?" said Mr. Murdoch, in a whisper like the coldest wind.

The boy made a noise, half-croak, half-squeak, and looked down at the floor. An astonishing change suddenly came over Mr. Murdoch's face. His mouth flew open wide in a kind of triumphant leer. At the same time he winked broadly at the class, which laughed uproariously. The boy looked up, bewildered, and Mr. Murdoch was forced to snap his mouth closed like a lizard snapping on a fly. This caused another burst of laughter.

Every student in Queen Anne School, when they finally reached sixth grade, was surprised and relieved to discover that their math teacher, Mr. Murdoch, looked fierce by mistake. His torture sessions were nothing but a little joke that he and the sixth grade at Queen Anne played on all the other students. Mr. Murdoch wasn't fierce at all. He was enthusiastic, confused, confusing, and unfailingly cheerful about mathematics.

Nevertheless, Erin couldn't help but feel sorry for his victims. She herself was still frightened of Mr. Murdoch, although in a different way. Mr. Murdoch expected Erin to follow what he was doing on the board, and she hardly ever did. When that happened, Erin began to feel panicky, as if she didn't belong in the school with normal kids but should be in a special institution somewhere with all the other vegetables.

The only thing she really liked about Mr. Murdoch

was that he let people whisper together as they worked, and that made the classes just bearable. It allowed Erin to share her recent problem with her deskmate, Sherry Salisky.

"Take the job," said Sherry. She looked up at the board and began to carefully copy the next problem into her book. Sherry was tiny and pretty, with tight blond curls. She looked as if she belonged in third grade or in a fairy-tale book, tasting porridge. Unlike Erin, who didn't have a clue what she wanted to be when she grew up, Sherry already knew she was going to be prime minister of the country, or at the very least premier of the province. Sherry was working hard enough to make it, and Erin was delighted to sit beside her in math. She looked over at Sherry's notebook and began to copy the last problem that Sherry had completed, including the answer, into her own book.

"It's easy for you to say," said Erin. "You're treated like an adult at home. Nobody tells you what to do after school." This wasn't quite true, but Sherry liked to pretend it was. Her mother got home from work at seven in the evening, and her father even later. Sherry spent her afternoons and evenings at the Dartmouth Public Library, studying hard, partly because she wanted to and partly because she had to. Sherry was doing very well in school, but she didn't have much fun during the week. Erin didn't envy her, except possibly when it came to doing math.

Sherry glanced over at Erin and scowled with annoyance when she saw that Erin was carefully copying her work. "For heaven's sake, Erin, try to do some yourself. They're easy!"

Just what everyone always says, thought Erin. She was forced to copy the next problem from the board, since Sherry was holding up the side of her notebook to prevent Erin from seeing.

The problems were all on the addition of mixed fractions, like $\frac{1}{3} + \frac{3}{4}$. Erin really should have spoken up two days ago, when they had just started and she couldn't follow a word of what Mr. Murdoch was saying. But everyone else seemed to understand, and Mr. Murdoch, as always, was beaming with delight and saying over and over again, "Isn't it easy?" Erin didn't want to make a fool of herself so she said nothing, hoping as she always hoped that there would be a sudden flash of light and she would understand. For a while she seemed to be doing something right to the fractions and getting some correct answers. But now, two days later, the problems were harder and she was hopelessly lost. As usual.

Erin jumped as Mr. Murdoch's voice abruptly sounded just behind her. The torture session was over, the victim released, and Mr. Murdoch was prowling the class as he often did. But mercifully, he had pounced on Sherry.

"You've got the method right, Sherry, but where's your arithmetic gone? Three times two is?" Sherry looked embarrassed. She had added instead of multiplied. Erin glanced over as Sherry furiously erased a five from one of her earlier problems and replaced it with a six.

Erin glanced down at her work and realized with horror that she had copied the same childish arithmetic mistake. In the same moment hateful Mr. Murdoch's voice said, "Let's see how you're doing, Erin."

Of course he had to notice, and he did. He picked up Erin's notebook and dramatically turned to the front page.

"Astounding!" he said. "It says Erin McEwan here. I would have expected it to say Sherry Salisky. I'm glad to see you don't have to copy your name from someone else, at least." The class laughed and Erin felt humiliated, as she so often did in math class. Was Mr. Murdoch actually going to get angry, for once? No, he just pressed his thin lips together and shook his head from side to side. Then he sighed and handed back her notebook.

"Perhaps it's the best thing, Erin. You go ahead and keep on copying," he said. "I've said all I'm going to say this year to you. Perhaps next year you and I can make a fresh start. With just a little bit of cooperation from you, and an extra year to study, I'm sure you'll find out just how easy math can be."

Now the class was silent. Erin almost wished they would laugh at her again. Instead all she felt were dozens of silent, pitying eyes. Was this the end of the line? Had Mr. Murdoch just told her it was certain—that she was going to have to take the grade over again?

"Sorry," whispered Sherry after a few moments.

"What are you sorry for?" said Erin from between clenched teeth. She was tracing the number four over and over again with her pencil, while she was trying to burn a hole in the paper with her eyes and wishing that it was Mr. Murdoch's skin.

"Listen, why don't you come with me to the library every day after school and study?" said Sherry.

"What's the point?" said Erin. "You heard what he said. As far as he's concerned, I've already failed." Then suddenly she had an idea. If she had already failed, then really she didn't need to worry about her math homework, and in that case . . .

"Sherry, would you do me an extra-special favor?" she whispered.

"Are you sure you wouldn't mind, Sherry?" said Erin's mother. It was lunchtime and the two girls were both breathless. They had quickly eaten their lunch at school, then had half-run, half-walked all the way to Erin's house, twenty minutes away.

"No," said Sherry.

Erin's mother frowned. "I wish you looked more convinced," she said.

"No, I'm convinced," said Sherry doubtfully. Erin, who was standing behind her mother, looked daggers at Sherry, who gave a sort of a smile.

"Anyway, Sherry's not my keeper," said Erin. "I could go to the library every day even if Sherry wasn't there."

"Well, I don't want you there on your own, Erin. I don't mind you working with a girl with sense enough to study, like Sherry. Just fooling around the library all afternoon on your own is out of the question."

"Mother, I solemnly promise you, if Sherry isn't at the library, I won't stay there either." It was a really easy promise to make, because Erin did not plan to be at the library at all.

"I'll love you forever for this, Sherry," said Erin as she spread her books out on the library table opposite her friend.

"I still don't know if you're doing the right thing, Erin," said Sherry.

"You're the one who said I should take the job," Erin reminded her. "As long as you help me, I can take it."

"But you're going to have to do *some* homework," said Sherry.

"Relax. I will. After I get home. But there's really no point in going crazy trying to study if Mr. Murdoch's going to fail me anyway, is there?" Even Sherry had to admit that it didn't make much sense.

"Right now it's more important to get my Mom's job back," she said. "Wait for me, and we'll walk home together." She gave Sherry a quick hug and rushed off out the door and down the hill toward the harbor and the ferry.

5

What was going on behind the counter? Wrestling? And why was a customer in a coat behind there too? "Oh, Erin!" shrieked Mrs. Sbrocchi. "Thank God you're here!" She rushed out from behind the counter, her hair askew and face anxious. She ripped off her apron with one hand and seized Erin's arm.

"Mrs. Eberhardt has cut the tip of her finger off with the meat slicer!" she said, pulling Erin to the cash register.

"This is the button that opens the cash drawer," she said. "I've got to take her to the hospital. Can you clean up the blood? You're not squeamish, are you? Push the button to—"

Mrs. Eberhardt herself interrupted this stream of instructions and questions. She was sitting on the chair behind the counter, supported by the customer, looking even paler than usual. She said, "For heaven's sake, Mrs. Sbrocchi. It isn't that serious. It's just a bit of flesh off the very tip."

But Mrs. Sbrocchi was determined that only her driving could get Mrs. Eberhardt to the hospital before she died. "I thought we'd have to close up! You can make change, can't you, Erin?"

Erin nodded. She wasn't a complete fool.

"Good," said Mrs. Sbrocchi. "But don't try to ring anything up on the cash register. If you have any trouble, go next door to the dress boutique." And with this last volley of instructions she assisted a shaky-looking Mrs. Eberhardt through the door and was gone. Erin was in charge.

Help! What do I do now? thought Erin. The familiar store suddenly seemed forbidding. Important things were always taken care of by someone else. Erin knew how to clean up, how to wash dishes, how to stock shelves. But actually selling things! She had only the haziest notion of how to run an Italian–German–Nova Scotian cookcraft gourmet delicatessen and takeout catering service.

Well, okay, she thought. I might as well get on with the things I can do, like cleaning up. A trail of blood led from the meat slicer across the counter. That definitely needed cleaning up. Blessing the fact that there were no customers, she began to scrub the counter.

After finishing the counter she eyed the meat slicer. It was obviously dangerous, and she had been told before to stay away from it. What about the neat pile of corned beef on the table in front of the circular blade? Since it probably was hiding a slice of finger, Erin doubted that anyone would be particularly happy to buy it, even if it was marked down. She carefully swept the meat onto a square of waxed paper, then dropped it into the garbage. She had unplugged the slicer and was still cautiously washing it when her first customer came in.

Go get a jar from the shelves, prayed Erin. But the customer, a very short, silver-haired gentleman, approached the cabinet filled with cheeses and preserved meats beside the cash register instead.

"Hello?" said the man after a moment, looking around. Erin reluctantly moved so that she wasn't screened by a large basket of bagels.

"Can I help you?" she said.

"Is that all of you?" said the man with a smile. He had a German or Polish accent. "Or you're maybe standing in a hole?"

"We've had an accident," explained Erin. "I'm just helping out."

"Good," said the man. "I'll have about six ounces of headcheese, please."

It was the worst possible request.

She looked frantically at the list of cheeses on the wall behind her, searching for a price.

"I'm afraid we don't have any," she said.

"Come down to my level," he said. He had squatted and was looking into the cabinet through the glass. On the other side of the cabinet Erin stooped down as well and peered at the customer over the meats and cheeses.

"It's right under your nose," he said, pointing to a roll of jellied meat.

"That's meat," said Erin.

"Don't argue with your customers," said the man. "Look on the list there."

So Erin looked at the meat list. And there it was: HEADCHEESE: $3.75/lb.

"Oh," she said, and stood there.

"Aren't you going to sell me some?" he asked.

"The prices are in pounds," explained Erin. "You wanted ounces. I'm not very good at multiplication. Or is it division?"

"It's neither; it's weighing. You put it on the scale and the scale does all the work."

"Oh," said Erin. That sounded like the right way to do math—with machines. But still she stood there.

"What is it, miss?" said the man after a moment. He flashed a good-humored smile. "You don't serve people shorter than you are?" He was indeed a very short man.

"I don't know how to use the meat slicer," she said. "Besides, it just sliced off the tip of somebody's finger."

"Serves them right," said the old gentleman. "Fingers don't belong anywhere near meat slicers. Let me show you."

"I don't think—" said Erin. But before she could stop him, he had slipped around the counter and was taking off his coat.

"Don't worry, my dear," he said, patting her on the

arm. "I was a butcher before I retired." The man went straight to the sink and started to wash his hands.

"Have you washed your hands?" he said to Erin.

"I only got here two minutes before you did," said Erin.

"No excuses. Wash them," he said, as if he was in charge of the store, not Erin.

She washed them.

"And if you're to be handling money too, you'll have to keep on washing them," he said as he slid open the display case and pulled out the headcheese.

Then he showed Erin how to set the meat on the movable table of the meat counter, and how it was held in place with the heavy lever arm. Erin knew enough to place a piece of waxed paper on the other side of the blade to catch the slices.

"Good," he said, and he turned on the machine. The circular blade whirled ominously. Erin took a step back. "Just the right thing to do," said the man. "Let it work by itself. It doesn't need your fingers to help." And sure enough, the table with the meat on it was slowly moving closer to the blade.

"Could I have a quarter pound of corned beef, please?" said a woman's voice. They both turned. They had been so absorbed in the lesson that they hadn't noticed the second customer. The man looked at Erin, then stepped back.

"Go ahead," he said. "I'll watch you."

So Erin turned the machine off. With a little help from the woman, she located the corned beef. She placed it cautiously in the machine and started it again.

"Thinner slices for this," said the man, and showed Erin the dial to turn to control the thickness of the slices. Then they both watched, mesmerized, as corned beef piled up on the butcher's paper.

"Whoa! Whoa!" called the man finally. "How are you going to tell when you've got a quarter pound?"

Erin shrugged. The man rolled his eyes.

"What do they teach you kids in school these days?" He switched off the machine and threw the waxed paper laden with corned beef on the scale beside the meat slicer.

"Now what?" he prompted.

Erin shrugged again, feeling foolish. Exasperated, the man showed her the pound price marked on the board, then showed her how to punch it into the keyboard on the scale.

"The scale does all the arithmetic," said the man. "Not like in my day. I had to do it. Now put slices on or take them off until you get a quarter pound. No, not in that window, that's the price window. This one," he said, tapping the pounds window of the electronic scale. But the scale showed decimals, not fractions, and Erin was uncertain about how decimals and fractions changed themselves back and forth.

"I'll do the meat," said the man finally, after exchanging glances with the woman across the counter. He swiftly wrapped up the meat in the paper, taped it, and wrote the price on the outside. Erin felt helpless.

"And a small tub of the Greek salad," said the woman. "Oh, and some bread." She looked around for it.

"The bread's just around that corner," said Erin, pointing, happy that at last she could actually do something useful. And she could manage the salad, spooning it carefully into a little plastic tub and sealing it. Fortunately there was no weighing involved since the salads were priced according to three sizes of containers. Now we're starting to move, she thought to herself proudly.

But then she was faced with meat, and a salad, and a loaf of rye bread. She hesitated.

"Well, go on," said the man. "Ring them in."

"Mrs. Sbrocchi told me not to," she said, staring at a bewildering array of keys, including ones with little department tags that said things like DAIRY and BOOKS on them.

"Then use a piece of paper," said the man, ever helpful. He looked under the counter and promptly came up with a pad. There was a pencil attached to the cash register by a string. Erin picked it up slowly. There was suddenly a horrible smell in the air. The smell of math class. The smell of failure.

"You *can* add?" said the man, noticing her hesitation.

"Of course I can," said Erin. But she simply stared at the piece of paper, doing nothing. After a moment the woman sighed loudly and looked at her watch.

"What is the problem?" asked the man gently.

"I can add," she said. "But I never seem to get the same answer everyone else does."

"Can you make change?" he said.

"Yes," she said positively. Making change only involved a single subtraction—taking what you were owed from what you were handed. She was sure she could manage that.

"I tell you what," said the man, pulling over the pad and beginning to quickly jot down prices. "I'm not in such a big hurry. I'll handle the meat and the adding. You handle the money and everything else." And they did.

It became busier than usual for a late Wednesday afternoon, so Erin was astonished when Mr. Przbylski (he had told her his name—even spelled it—but she still couldn't pronounce it) said, "It's five past six, Erin. You don't stay open past six, do you?" And they tried the bundle of keys in the cash register, and found the one that locked the doors, and that was that.

When the manager and assistant manager finally arrived and knocked on the window at six thirty, Mr. Przbylski was gone and Erin was trying her very best to add up the cash.

"I lost my head. I should never have left you on your own," said Mrs. Sbrocchi, giving Erin a hug and praising her to the heavens and beyond. Mrs. Eberhardt, even with her one bandaged finger, quickly rang all of

Erin's sales into the register and added up the cash.

"Look at you. The law says you're too young even to have a job, and here you ran a whole store for an hour and a half. Amazing!" said Mrs. Sbrocchi as they did the dishes together.

Erin grinned.

"I'm really pleased that your parents changed their minds. Do you suppose I should call and—"

"No," said Erin hastily.

"No, I guess you're right. We'd better leave things well enough alone for a while."

On her way back on the ferry Erin sat up top, enjoying the warm evening. Tonight there was a touch of summer in the air. The sun was sinking low behind the Halifax shore, and across the harbor the houses and buildings of Dartmouth were tinged with the first hints of an orange sunset.

It had been a good first day, and for a while Erin was quite pleased with herself. Not only had she looked after the store, but she had actually done some math successfully. For nearly two hours she had made change.

When Mrs. Eberhardt had finished adding up all the money in the till and comparing it to the cash register tape, she had called out, "We're short a dollar twenty-two."

For a moment Erin's stomach had tightened with familiar fears. Another math test. Another math failure. But to her surprise, Mrs. Sbrocchi said, "That's all? That's normal. Well done, Erin." Normal? Erin? In math? It was an all-new feeling, and Erin quite liked it. She had found out that the store was always over or under a few cents in the till by the end of the day. "Mind you, that's a dollar twenty-two all day, Erin. Not just when you were here. You might have been perfect." Perfect? Well, let's not get carried away.

So it was just possible that Erin might actually learn some math at the store, as Mrs. Sbrocchi had promised. At least, if she kept on doing the job.

But after a while the glow began to wear off and Erin found herself worrying again. For once, though, she was not worrying about the events of the past few days, but her own future.

Until this afternoon math had been nothing more than a terrible annoyance at school. Avoiding math had meant trouble in school, extra homework, even repeating a year. But on this one afternoon she had suddenly realized that math could be very important *outside* of school. Suddenly math had become very real. The fact that she was so bad at it was frightening.

She had planned to share her triumph with Sherry as they walked home together. But by the time she arrived back at the library, Erin was quiet, thinking. When Sherry said once again, just before turning off for her house, "I still think you should try to do some math homework, sometime," Erin found herself agreeing.

But when?

6

"What's that?" said Mrs. Eberhardt suspiciously, poking at a limp green bunch on the counter as if it might leap up and grab her by the throat. Erin looked over from where she was rearranging jars of pickles in the cooler.

It was just after four, the evening rush had not yet begun, and she and Mrs. Eberhardt were alone together. Mrs. Eberhardt was clutching a damp plastic bag between two elegant fingers. In the other hand she held a tomato-salad recipe scrawled by Mrs. Sbrocchi.

"And this time *exactly* according to my recipe," she had instructed.

Yesterday Mrs. Eberhardt had been told to make potato salad. She had been given a recipe for that, too. The old beams in the store were still ringing with the shrieks of rage that had come from Mrs. Sbrocchi when she tasted the potato salad and discovered that Mrs. Eberhardt had changed the recipe.

"It was too oniony," protested Mrs. Eberhardt.

"This place was built on *my* cooking," Mrs. Sbrocchi

56

had roared. "And don't tell me that your famous degree from the university was a Bachelor of Salads!"

"It was a Bachelor of Commerce," said Mrs. Eberhardt with a sniff.

"Ha!"

"But I did raise a family," said Mrs. Eberhardt weakly. "And feed them."

"On what? TV dinners?" Mrs. Sbrocchi called as she dumped the whole huge bowl of salad into the sink with a *glop* and turned on the garbage disposal.

This time, Mrs. Eberhardt was determined to follow the recipe to the letter. But what exactly was this bag of green stuff?

"Erin dear, could you come over here a minute?" she said.

Erin scowled. She did not like being called "dear" by Mrs. Eberhardt. But it was her job to help out, so reluctantly she went.

"Do you have any idea what this is?" said Mrs. Eberhardt.

"Yup," said Erin. And she did. It was an herb, no question about it. She tore off a piece of leaf and popped it into her mouth.

"Yum," said Erin. "It's—" But her memory wasn't cooperating. It was sharp and tangy and wonderful. "It's delicious," she said finally, and Mrs. Eberhardt frowned at her in annoyance, as if Erin was deliberately being difficult.

"Well, it isn't basil," said Mrs. Eberhardt firmly.

Of course, that's what it was. "Yes, it is," said Erin.

Mrs. Eberhardt broke off a corner of a leaf and popped it in her mouth. "Eugh," she said. "That's nothing like basil."

She looked again at the recipe in her hand. "So far as I can tell from Mrs. Sbrocchi's dreadful handwriting, it says 'cup of basil top right cooler.' And this green stuff was the only thing on the top right that wasn't a bottle."

She looked at it again, then shook her head. "It must be a mistake," she said finally.

Erin shrugged. If Mrs. Eberhardt didn't want to take Erin's word for it, well, that was her business.

Mrs. Eberhardt dipped gracefully under the counter and started off down the aisle toward the spice rack. "She must have meant top right spice rack." She stood in front of the rack and studied it for a moment, then said, "Aha!"

Triumphantly she held up a little bottle. "And that's where it is, just where it should be, on the top right of the spice rack." She unscrewed the cap and poured a pinch into her palm as she returned. She leaned over the counter and offered it to Erin.

"What does that taste like to you?" she said.

"Dried grass," said Erin, trying to spit the little bits off her tongue.

"Well, I'm afraid your mother hasn't taught you

58

everything quite yet, my dear." She tasted a pinch herself. "It tastes like basil to me, and its says basil on the bottle. You can carry on now."

"Mrs. Sbrocchi gets all her herbs fresh from a greenhouse in—" Erin started to say. But Mrs. Eberhardt had everything under control now, and was paying no attention to Erin as she ducked under the counter and began to study the recipe anew.

Erin shrugged again and returned to the cooler, where she began to damp-mop the sides with vinegar and water. Over at the counter she heard Mrs. Eberhardt murmur to herself, "A whole cup? Well, ours is not to reason why."

For a moment Erin watched Mrs. Eberhardt and imagined her mother in the same place. What a contrast! Mrs. McEwan whizzed about the kitchen like a small top. When she picked up a fork, it became a whirring extension of her arm. Mrs. Eberhardt in the kitchen reminded Erin of a swan out of water, all her graceful beauty destroyed by awkward movements. Her elbow stuck out and her long, graceful neck jerked and lurched as she stabbed her mixing spoon in and out of a bowl.

As Erin watched out of the corner of her eye, Mrs. Eberhardt returned to the spice rack for more dried basil. This she dumped, bottle after bottle, into the salad. With every bottle Erin paused in her cleaning and winced with delight.

At first Mrs. Sbrocchi didn't notice the new salad, hidden among a dozen others in the display case. When she returned, the shop had grown busy, and she plunged into the business of serving customers.

Erin, meanwhile, was caught at the back of the store at the big dairy cooler, practicing some real math, fortunately a very easy kind. She was slowly recounting all the yogurts and sour creams that the yogurt deliveryman had already counted. He looked slightly annoyed, but Erin did her best to ignore him. She was acting under strict orders from Mrs. Sbrocchi.

"Never trust deliverymen, no matter how nice they are, and you'll always get along fine with them," Mrs. Sbrocchi had said, adding, "And you won't lose any money, either."

At long last Erin was finished. She stood up straight, and for a moment said nothing. She had a problem.

"Well?" said the deliveryman. He stood there tapping his pencil on a clipboard and looking exasperated.

"Gosh, I'm sorry," said Erin. "I must have counted wrong. I count six fewer strawberry yogurts than you do." She did not say it with a great deal of confidence. It was only adding by ones, but she was so used to being wrong at math that it was probably her fault.

The deliveryman frowned, and rapidly recounted. Then he paused and his frown deepened. He didn't say anything, but it appeared that he just might have reached the same wrong number as Erin. He began to shuffle all the varieties of yogurt around looking for more strawberries, until finally, when the case was a sea of confusion, he said, "Here they are."

"No, those were here before," said Erin confidently. She knew exactly what was where in this cooler. To prove it, she showed him the date stamped on the yogurt. It was earlier than on the new ones.

"Gosh darn, I'm sorry," said the driver. "This only ever happens when I'm running late." Erin gave him a cool smile which hid the fact that inside she was jumping up and down with joy. A math contest with an adult and I won! she thought.

The man went out to the truck for more yogurt. When he came back, an extra package of yogurt tucked under his arm, he paused at the counter and offered the clipboard to Mrs. Sbrocchi. But she just said something and waved to Erin.

He arrived back at the dairy cooler looking embarrassed and said, "Mrs. Sbrocchi said you counted them, you sign for them." So Erin, feeling a little frightened at the responsibility and terribly important, signed her name at the bottom of the invoice in her best handwriting. Then she accepted a copy and another apology with a gracious bend of her head, just as she had seen the Grand Duchess Eberhardt do.

A few moments later, bending over to unscramble the mess of yogurts, she received a sharp slap on the bottom that almost tipped her into the cooler.

"Oh!" she squeaked.

"That's my girl," said Mrs. Sbrocchi. "See, you *can*

do the counting when it counts." Then, as Erin pulled herself out of the yogurt, Mrs. Sbrocchi bustled up to the front of the store.

A moment later Erin heard the roar of her voice. All conversation in the store ceased. "What's *that?*" said Mrs. Sbrocchi again, no more quietly than the first time. Erin crept forward to watch as Mrs. Eberhardt said timidly, "Just what you asked me to make, Mrs. Sbrocchi."

"I asked for tomato salad," thundered Mrs. Sbrocchi, sweeping behind the counter and reaching into the big display case. She pulled out a square stainless steel container filled with tomato slices half hidden in a brown sludge. "What do you call this? Cartwheels in hay?" There was a snicker from some of the customers, who were beginning to edge into a ring around the scene like a bunch of gawking bystanders at a traffic accident. Erin crept up between them.

Mrs. Eberhardt watched anxiously as Mrs. Sbrocchi forked a slice of tomato out of the salad and rather messily crammed it into her mouth.

"Phwoo!" said Mrs. Sbrocchi, spitting wildly into the sink. For a while she choked and gagged, much to the delight of her audience—with the exception of the woeful Mrs. Eberhardt.

"Are you trying to poison my customers?" said Mrs. Sbrocchi. "I couldn't give this away to pigs."

"I followed your recipe—"

"Followed? Where's the fresh basil?"

"Fresh? Well, I . . . I've never . . . I didn't . . ."

62

"Erin, where's Erin?" said Mrs. Sbrocchi, wildly pointing her finger around the store. Erin stepped forward reluctantly. "I hold you responsible for this, Erin! Mrs. Eberhardt doesn't know her bottom from a beehive. But *you* know! Why didn't you show her the fresh basil?"

Erin opened her mouth and closed it again. There was no point in saying anything. Mrs. Sbrocchi was just like her mother. When they got steamed up, they never listened. Anyway, she knew Mrs. Sbrocchi didn't really blame her. Erin tried to make her face as solemn as possible and to look sorry about everything. But it was difficult because inside she was positively delighted as she watched Mrs. Eberhardt's latest salad disappear, *kafloop*, into the sink. The way things were going, Mrs. Eberhardt was going to end up getting fired, and her mother was sure to get her job back. What with that, and outcounting the deliveryman, it had turned out to be a really good day. A good day for her, anyway, if not for Mrs. Eberhardt and, it seemed, for Mrs. Sbrocchi.

After the store had closed and all the chores were finished, Erin came back to collect her coat and found the owner frowning over her glasses at a little haystack of invoices.

"Anything wrong?" said Erin.

"Mmm," said Mrs. Sbrocchi. She shook her head in annoyance. "For some reason, I seem to be making too much money."

"Seriously?" said Erin with a laugh.

But Mrs. Sbrocchi surprised her by frowning. "It's not a joke, Erin. I seem to have made too much money this month, and I can't figure out why."

"Gee, I'm sorry," said Erin, and said good-bye. She wasn't really sorry at all. She couldn't understand how Mrs. Sbrocchi could be upset about making too much money all of a sudden. That was one problem that Erin personally was not going to spend much time worrying about!

At seven Erin arrived at the library, all out of breath from running up the hill from the ferry. As Erin crossed the library toward Sherry, her friend looked up. She looked strangely worried. Erin soon found out why.

"Your father was just in here," said Sherry.

"Oh no!" groaned Erin, and all the good news that she was planning to report crumbled out of her mind.

"It's all right," said Sherry with a proud smile. "I fixed it."

"How?" said Erin, feeling limp.

"I said you were in the bathroom. He only came in to get a book. I asked him to wait, but he said that he sees enough of you as it is, and he wasn't going to wait for the thrill of seeing you *yet* again."

"Is that the way he said it?" said Erin.

"Yup. He was in a good mood."

Erin slumped down in her chair with relief. It had been a close call.

7

It was nice to be good at making change and counting yogurt. But Erin didn't have many opportunities at Sbrocchi's to do either. And it really wasn't very complicated mathematics anyway, nothing that would help her in her sixth-grade schoolwork. After several days Erin began to wonder if Mrs. Sbrocchi really was going to help her with her math. This worry grew just a little larger each night as Erin arrived home, quite exhausted. She had to face her out-of-work mother, who was doing her best to be cheerful but not always succeeding. At that late hour Erin also had to face her homework, which nobody but Erin knew had not even been touched.

"I must say I'm surprised," said her mother, seeing Erin at the kitchen table with her nose in her English homework. "And pleased, of course," she added as she hustled Erin off to bed. "Four hours of homework at the library *and* another hour and a half at home. I'd love to see you at the top of your class, but not by having you do without sleep."

What with her mother pushing her off to bed, Erin had been having trouble getting any homework done. Of course, she always left math for last. It always seemed to be the very next thing to do just as she was sent to bed. When Erin grew tired, she began to wonder whether there was really any point in doing *any* homework in *any* subject. Seeing as she was probably going to fail anyway.

And though she was worried that Mrs. Sbrocchi *wouldn't* help her with math, she was also worried that Mrs. Sbrocchi *would*.

Erin was very fond of Mrs. Sbrocchi, the friend. And she was getting along well with Mrs. Sbrocchi, the boss. But Erin was growing just a little bit nervous about Mrs. Sbrocchi, the teacher. After all, she had spent three days watching Mrs. Sbrocchi, the teacher, teaching Mrs. Eberhardt, the slow learner, how to cook. It was not a pretty sight.

Shortly after she arrived on Friday afternoon she heard the determined clatter of Mrs. Sbrocchi's feet behind her. A hand grabbed the sleeve of her blouse and began to tow her along.

"You come with me, little Miss McPighead," said Mrs. Sbrocchi. "It's time you learned a little math."

So there was going to be math after all. "Like what?" said Erin nervously as she was led toward the office door.

"Markups, markdowns, discounts, that kind of thing," said Mrs. Sbrocchi cheerfully.

"Gee, I don't know," said Erin, stopping outside the office. "I don't think we do that this year in school."

Mrs. Sbrocchi turned to Erin with an exaggerated expression of surprise on her face. "You don't *do* markups?" she said. Then she turned to the store, which was empty except for poor Mrs. Eberhardt, who was sweating behind the counter over the preparation of salad.

"Hold everything!" cried Mrs. Sbrocchi. "No markups!" She went sweeping down the aisle waving theatrically at everything. "Sell everything at cost price. Erin doesn't *do* markups."

Mrs. Eberhardt, concentrating, could only spare a thin smile.

"So!" cried Mrs. Sbrocchi. "Sbrocchi's goes out of business. All because"—she dropped her voice as the tinkling of a bell announced the arrival of a customer in the shop—"Erin McEwan doesn't do markups in sixth grade."

"That's not . . . I didn't mean . . ." began Erin, but Mrs. Sbrocchi seized her arm firmly and towed her into the office.

"Erin," she said. "There are no grades out here in the real world. When you need to do it, that's when you learn to do it. I don't care if they don't teach markups until university." She closed the door behind her firmly.

"Doesn't Mrs. Eberhardt . . . ?" said Erin, making

one last try to wriggle out. "I mean, I'm sure she could probably do them better."

"I'm sure she could," said Mrs. Sbrocchi, approaching her spotless desk. "What she can't do better at the moment is salads, and that is what I want her to work on." She plumped herself down in her chair and drew Erin close to her.

"She's out there making a Greek salad," said Mrs. Sbrocchi, speaking in a hoarse whisper. "The trouble is, she doesn't like the taste of raw onions. She doesn't like the taste of olive oil, or olives, or feta cheese." She snorted and rolled her eyes. "Now how can you prepare food if you don't like the taste of it?"

She sighed and swept her arm around her. "I swear I've made a mistake. And look what she's done to my office." To Erin, it seemed unreasonable to complain about the neatness. The office-storeroom was now in perfect order, with the food on the shelves organized in neat rows. During the winter when Erin had come in to help her mother it had always been difficult trying to find extra jars of jelly or cans of seafood to put out on the shelves.

"Mrs. Eberhardt trained to be an accountant," grumbled Mrs. Sbrocchi. "So of course she feels she has a perfect right to meddle with all my books and bills and checks, and as if that wasn't enough, all this unnecessary rearranging of the shelves so that I can't find—you haven't seen my umbrella recently, have you, Erin?"

"No," said Erin.

"Exactly," said Mrs. Sbrocchi. "It's all her fault."

Erin looked closely at Mrs. Sbrocchi. Was she *really* annoyed? Erin knew that Mrs. Sbrocchi was a very sensible person at heart. Was something else the matter?

She looked closely at Mrs. Sbrocchi, who seemed to sense what Erin was thinking.

"Oh, I know I sound unreasonable," she said. "But I can't for the life of me find out why I've made so much money this month."

Erin rolled her eyes. Poor, rich Mrs. Sbrocchi!

The owner caught Erin's look and laughed. "Yes, I know it sounds silly, but it's nagging. Mrs. Eberhardt has so rearranged all my papers that I can't figure out what's happened."

Mrs. Sbrocchi rapidly pulled books and paper from various drawers and spread them in a comfortable mess around the top of the desk. "Right," she said. She held up a piece of paper. "This is an invoice from one of our customers. You know what an invoice is?"

"Sort of a bill?" said Erin.

"Sort of exactly," said Mrs. Sbrocchi. "It tells us what they sent us . . . here." She ran her pencil down a column of strange abbreviations: names like "gr ga jam" and "mxd must pick Kelly's."

"Finished?" said Mrs. Sbrocchi impatiently as Erin held the invoice in front of her and studied it.

"Not really," said Erin. It was fun trying to puzzle out the abbreviations. It was also a good way of avoiding the long columns of numbers beside the abbreviations.

Mrs. Sbrocchi finally got fed up and muscled the invoice away from Erin. "Number of items," she said, running her pencil down the first column of numbers beside the abbreviations. "Kind of item," said Mrs. Sbrocchi. This was another column in blessed English, not numbers, which said "doz" or "jars" or other words like that.

"Got it," said Erin.

"Fine. Now, these columns are two of the most important. This column is wholesale price per item, and this column is suggested retail price. Clear?"

"Er . . ." said Erin, as if she had just been introduced to a cage full of hairy-toed fruit wombats. She knew that a wombat was an animal, just as she knew that a wholesale price was a price. Of some sort. But what sort?

"Wholesale is the price I buy at," said Mrs. Sbrocchi. "Retail is the price I sell at. The difference is the markup. Okay?"

Erin studied the cage of wombats carefully.

Finally Mrs. Sbrocchi ran her pencil along one line and said, "Mixed mustard pickles, six dozen—that's seventy-two—at one twenty wholesale and one eighty retail." She stopped before she got to the last column, filled with the biggest numbers, and Erin didn't care to ask what it meant.

"Okay," said Erin cautiously.

"You see the two prices, wholesale and retail, are different?"

70

"Uh-huh."

"What would happen if they were the same?" said Mrs. Sbrocchi.

Erin thought for a while. "It would be much easier to figure out," she said finally.

"Erin! For heaven's sake!" exploded Mrs. Sbrocchi. "I'd be out of business! Suppose I bought a jar of olives from Mrs. Eberhardt and sold it to you for exactly the same price. Why would I bother?"

"I don't know," said Erin. "I don't like olives."

Mrs. Sbrocchi lowered her head to the desk and banged it slowly several times. "Whether you like olives or not," said Mrs. Sbrocchi. "I have to buy them from Mrs. Eberhardt for one price and sell them to you for a higher price, or I won't be able to afford to pay rent on the store or make a salary. See?"

Erin thought she saw.

"And the difference between the two—you admit there *has* to be a difference—is the markup. See?"

Erin thought she saw that, too.

"Wonderful," said Mrs. Sbrocchi. "Don't worry about the last column for the moment. That's the wholesale price I pay for all seventy-two jars.

"So let's review it. Item, pickles. One jar I buy wholesale for, say, x. I mark it up, say, forty-five percent and sell it retail for x plus forty-five percent."

Mrs. Sbrocchi didn't say "Clear?" this time, and Erin sorely wished she had. x? Forty-five percent? x plus forty-five percent? Where had all these ideas suddenly come

71

from, just as she was getting comfortable with the idea of buying for less and selling for more?

But Mrs. Sbrocchi was already scattering papers wildly about the desk. "Now, some of our suppliers don't suggest a retail price. And anyway, I might not want to sell at that price." She waved a new invoice under Erin's nose. "So we have to do the markups ourselves. Then, if we have a sale—which is exactly what we're going to have and why you and I are sitting here—then we have to discount our markup."

Before Erin could properly focus on the new invoice, it was whipped away and the old one was back. "So if our retail was, in this case, x plus forty-five percent, we would then discount it by, say, twenty percent off, so that our final selling price would be x plus forty-five percent first, then all of that less twenty percent. See?"

Mrs. Sbrocchi's explanation had long ago slipped into some strange dialect of Chinese and Erin didn't have the slightest idea what she was talking about. She wasn't helped by Mrs. Sbrocchi's enthusiastic scribblings all over scrap paper, which she filled with x's and %'s and other scorpionlike figures.

"Or we could write it like this," continued Mrs. Sbrocchi cheerfully. "One point four-five times wholesale times point eighty."

Well, all right, thought Erin miserably. Why not write it like that? Or maybe write it as "one zillion times the number of toes on a fruit wombat." Mrs. Sbrocchi was beginning to remind Erin strongly of her math teacher, Mr. Murdoch. They both seemed to get excited about numbers. They both scribbled messily all over the place using numbers you could hardly read. And they both seemed to pull numbers out of thin air. Where had one point four-five come from? And point eighty?

The lesson went quickly downhill after that. Erin discovered that in one way Mrs. Sbrocchi was different from Mr. Murdoch. She had a much worse temper.

After Erin had done her best to cover paper with numbers that didn't make much sense, Mrs. Sbrocchi stormed out, throwing the office door open with a crash. Several moments later there were some angry mutterings from the front of the store. Then Erin faintly heard a wet *kerflumping* sound. And was that the musical rattle of olives bouncing in the sink?

This time it was a Greek disaster. Another basin of Mrs. Eberhardt's salad on the way to the garbage disposal. Good. Things were one salad closer to her mother getting her job back. After what seemed like an eternity, there was a call from the front. "Where's the mop lady?"

Erin shot out of the room and attacked the floors, greatly relieved. After fifteen minutes of mopping and saying to herself, "Thank goodness I'm through" over and over again, she happened to glance up at the clock.

It said 7:40.

"Something is wrong with the clock," she said to Mrs.

73

Eberhardt, who was ringing up an order at the cash register.

Mrs. Eberhardt glanced up at it. "No, I don't think so, dear," she said with her hateful royal smile. And she went right on totaling up the order.

"But—" said Erin, confused.

"Looks right to me," said Mrs. Eberhardt's customer. He was a large man in a dark blue overcoat, with a beefy red face that went even redder as he forced back his sleeve to check his watch. "Yup, It's right," he said.

"But we close at six!" protested Erin.

Mrs. Eberhardt and Mrs. Sbrocchi laughed. "We close at nine on Fridays," said Mrs. Sbrocchi.

Erin was stunned. She'd always heard that time flies when you're having fun. Now she knew that time could fly when you're absolutely miserable and fighting with math.

"But I'll never make it home by eight!" said Erin. "They'll be calling the police and everything!"

"Ah," said Mrs. Sbrocchi, suddenly concerned. "Of course, your parents will be expecting you." It was a long way back to Dartmouth, and outside the windows the sky was tinged pink with the setting sun. "I'll call them and tell them I'll drive you home myself," she said, starting toward the office.

"No!" shouted Erin. Mrs. Sbrocchi stopped as if she had been shot dead, and a whole storeful of people looked up, startled.

"I mean yes!" said Erin, quickly starting for the back. "But I'll call. It was my fault for not noticing the time."

"No, no, Erin," said Mrs. Sbrocchi, catching Erin by the arm. "It was my fault for not thinking about it."

It turned into a wrestling match. In the end, it was the big beefy customer who came to her rescue. "If the little girl has the courage to face the music, I think it's admirable," he said. So Mrs. Sbrocchi gave in and let Erin phone.

If only they knew the truth, thought Erin as she reached the phone, then tried to spread herself out across the office as much as possible so that Mrs. Sbrocchi couldn't squeeze in beside her and listen.

She dialed as Mrs. Sbrocchi hovered anxiously in the doorway. Erin scowled at her in hopes she'd go away, but Mrs. Sbrocchi just scowled back in agreement at how serious it all was and nodded her head encouragingly.

In the end Erin was forced to turn her body so that the phone was hidden. She pushed her finger down on the button, cutting off the call.

"Hello?" she said. "Dad?"

Buzz went the phone.

"I'm sorry, I lost track of the time. The store doesn't close till nine. I hope you're not angry."

Buzz went the phone.

"Yes. Okay. I'll start home right away."

"I'm sorry, Mrs. Sbrocchi," explained Erin as she

struggled into her faded blue parka. "They don't want me out on my own so late. I can't work till nine."

She ran full speed up through the Historic Properties and along Water Street toward the ferry dock, hoping against hope that she could make the seven-forty-five ferry. She was thankful that she had at least managed to keep Mrs. Sbrocchi from phoning and finding out the truth. Her parents would absolutely murder her if she came home after eight.

She arrived breathless at the ferry just in time to see the ferry's lights slipping away from the dock.

"Oh no," she groaned. But there was nothing she could do to bring it back. So, her stomach churning, she sat on a bench and waited. A very long half hour later she was finally on her way. The sun had already disappeared behind the skyline of Halifax. Its last rays caught the bridge across the harbor together with houses and buildings at the top of the hills on the Dartmouth side. Erin remained outside, fidgeting on the top deck, unmindful of the rapidly cooling evening. She somehow felt that by staying out in the open and pacing up and down she could actually help the ferry move a little faster and delay the gathering darkness.

At eight thirty-two she panted up to the front doors of the library.

There, waiting, was a furious Sherry, clutching a

mountain of books. "You're an hour and a half late!" she said fiercely.

"I'm sorry," said Erin.

"I didn't know what to do!" raged Sherry. "I was really tempted to call your parents."

"No, don't do that," protested Erin as she collected her books and they started to hurry homeward. "Call the store first."

"You didn't give me the number," said Sherry angrily.

"You could have looked it up."

"Looked *what* up?"

"Sbrocchi."

"You never told me the name."

"Sure I did."

And so they had a fight for several blocks.

"My parents will be going crazy," muttered Sherry. "I'm supposed to be home at eight o'clock latest, just like you. They've probably phoned your parents already."

"That's okay," said Erin. "We're together, so they won't find out about me."

"Guess what? I wasn't thinking about you," said Sherry. "There are other people besides *you* around who can get into trouble."

"Sorry," said Erin for about the fiftieth time. "Anyway, it's not dark yet."

Sherry snorted.

Things weren't working out very well. The trouble was, Erin needed a favor from Sherry. They hurried together a few more minutes in silence until Erin finally said, "You didn't answer my question."

"What question?"

"Will you call and invite me over to play tomorrow? Saturday, remember?"

"Why?" said Sherry suspiciously.

"If my parents think I'm at your place, I can go to work tomorrow."

"No," said Sherry firmly. "Enough is enough." And no amount of pleading would change her mind.

By the time they split up Sherry was still angry with Erin and Erin had become angry with Sherry. They walked away from each other in gloomy silence, each preparing to face the music at home.

To Erin's astonishment, the music was pleasant.

"That you, Erin?" called her mother from the kitchen as Erin entered the front door. "Your dinner's frizzled." But it wasn't really. It was her mother's Italian meat loaf, and it was just as delicious as always. Mrs. McEwan had already eaten, but she sat opposite Erin and watched her daughter wolf down her food.

"Mrs. Salisky called in a lather about an hour ago," she said. "I told her you'd gone study crazy and not to worry till after the library closed."

"Thanks," said Erin.

"Nothing to thank me for," said her mother. "That

didn't cheer her up." Mrs McEwan laughed. "So I told her to call the desk at the library and describe the pair of you."

"Did she?"

"I told her to call me back if you weren't there. She didn't call, so I didn't worry. Although next time if you're going to stay later, *please* call me," she said, not very sternly. And that was all the trouble Erin got into for being late.

"How come you're so cheerful this evening?" said Erin.

"Ah, well, that would be telling," teased her mother.

"Come on."

"Well . . . I think I've got a job."

"No!" said Erin, spilling her milk all over the table in her excitement.

"Hold on, hold on," said her mother, frowning and wiping the table with a sponge. "I haven't got it yet."

"Whereabouts?"

"At the Royal Downtowner."

"In Halifax. Isn't that the big new hotel by the citadel?"

"Yup."

"Really? As a what?"

"A chef," said her mother proudly.

"A *real* chef?"

"Well, only doing desserts to start."

"But that's great!"

"And," said her mother, triumphantly playing her best card, "I already know the head chef. He used to come to Sbrocchi's and buy the odd thing. He's tried some of my cooking and he likes it.

"Wonderful!" said Erin, sweeping around the table to grab her mother and dance her around the kitchen.

That night, lying awake and staring at the comforting and still unpainted blotch on the ceiling, Erin began to feel strangely unsettled about her mother working again.

Erin had been disobeying her parents in a very serious way. And doing a great deal of lying. She had been doing an awful lot of homework dodging and was probably making it certain that she would fail her school year. While her family was in trouble, it all seemed to be the right thing to do.

But now, if her mother got a job, where would that leave Erin? At the very least, a year behind in school. Unless she somehow, some way, kept up with her schoolwork. As she fell asleep that night she promised herself that she would spend all day Sunday doing homework. She'd even do some math. Although, after making such a mess of Mrs. Sbrocchi's invoices, it was hard to believe she would ever master that impossible subject.

8

Who would have believed that it could be so hard to work on a Saturday? After all, there was no school, and Erin was allowed to do pretty much as she pleased. Except, it seemed, when it pleased her to disappear for eight hours. Erin hadn't really realized how closely her parents kept track of her. It seemed her friends had the same problem.

She made several whispered phone calls first thing on Saturday morning. They were all unsuccessful. Erin had several pretty good friends besides Sherry. She had been neglecting them lately, what with all her problems, and all of them were happy to have her over for the day. As long as she *really did* come over. And really stayed.

"What if your mom calls my mom looking for you?" they all said, one way or another.

"I'll be in trouble," said Erin.

"Me too," said voices at the other end of the phone line. None of these voices were interested in trouble. And that was that.

At eight thirty in the morning Erin's mother set out for Halifax to meet the chef at the Royal Downtowner. Erin's father, footsore from a night shift at the hospital, had just gone to bed. Erin was sitting in the living room, fresh out of ideas.

Then, at a quarter to nine, there was a lifesaving phone call. "It's the hospital," she said as she gently shook her father awake. "They've had three nursing assistants call in sick, and would you be interested in working today?"

"When you're a starving student, you jump at any chance you get," said Mr. McEwan as he staggered owl eyed and none too eager to the breakfast table, where Erin had coffee waiting for him.

So Erin, thanks to several sick nursing assistants, was left alone in the house. Her mother was gone: first the interview, then shopping and a visit with Erin's aunt in Halifax. Suddenly, nobody was checking up on Erin. She gave her father a fifteen-minute head start to the ferry, then followed.

"Sorry I'm late," she practiced as she sat in the sun on the top deck. It seemed that she was doing an awful lot of apologizing these days.

It was really and truly almost summerlike, a perfect late May morning. In the shelter of the pilothouse it was possible to practically bake in the sun. But even out of shelter the wind was warm. There were two sailboats out in the harbor, and the colored sail of a wind-surfer.

In the Historic Properties there were wanderers on the cobblestones, and just outside the door of Sbrocchi's was a sure sign of summer. There was Loaf.

Loaf's real name was Slice. Slice is a zippy name, suggesting speed and sharpness. But nobody called him Slice.

"He's not just one slice, he's the whole loaf," Mrs. Sbrocchi had explained the summer before.

And loaf was what Loaf did best. He was a large, fat, black, smelly Labrador retriever. All winter he loafed on the floor of the dress boutique next door to Sbrocchi's. All summer, he loafed just outside Sbrocchi's door, where he tripped unwary tourists. He was lying in the sun as Erin came upon him, wheezing in his sleep as he always did. The area around the doorway was perfumed with warm dog.

"Hello, Loaf," said Erin, and she bent down and picked up the large stainless steel mixing bowl that was resting by his head.

Loaf's body belonged to the dress shop, but his soul belonged to Mrs. Sbrocchi. Every day or so she would gather up scrap ends of meat and put them out for Loaf. Nobody ever bothered to point out that Loaf was overweight. After all, Mrs. Sbrocchi was overweight herself.

Erin checked the bowl and was not surprised to find that Loaf had licked it completely clean of little scraps of heaven. The bowl had been sitting in the sun and was positively hot. Erin carried it in the door.

"Sorry I'm late," she called. There were three customers at the front of the store who were pleased to forgive her, but nobody else was in sight. Erin plonked the bowl on the counter and headed back to the door of the office, which was closed.

Erin paused when she got to the door. Inside she could hear the faint sounds of an argument. It was music to her ears. Enough of these harsh words and Mrs. Eberhardt might be gone, and Mrs. McEwan reemployed.

Erin thought about that for a moment. She did feel just a little bit of sympathy for Mrs. Eberhardt. Anybody who had Mrs. Sbrocchi as a teacher deserved a *little* bit of sympathy. On the other hand, Mrs. Eberhardt was a rotten cook. Erin opened the door.

Mrs. Eberhardt wasn't a rotten bookkeeper, and that was what the fight was about. As the door opened, Erin heard Mrs. Eberhardt's angry voice say firmly, "I don't *care* if you want to teach children how to do books. I don't think it's fair to make a mess of all the invoices that I've spent hours—oh, Erin!"

"There are customers waiting," said Erin, wishing she was old enough and important enough to glare at them and speak with a snip in her voice just to let them know how childish they were being with all their arguing. The Grand Duchess Eberhardt swept out past her, leaving a frosting of icicles in the air and on the shelves. Somehow she left Erin feeling that the mess was all her fault.

Mrs. Sbrocchi had been sitting in her chair with her arms folded, looking stern. Now she motioned with her hand for Erin to close the door. She made a face, and Erin made one back. They both laughed and felt like scolded schoolchildren. But only for a moment.

"Sorry I'm late," said Erin. "I'll start the dishes." Mrs. Sbrocchi had obviously come in very early in morning to do some cooking. There was a mountain of pots and bowls by the sink and the whole shop was perfumed with the delicious smell of hot meat pies.

But Mrs. Sbrocchi had other plans for Erin. Horrible plans. "Come," she said, waving Erin to her side. "You've done enough dishes this week. I haven't forgotten my promise about math. Today is markups and discounts."

Again? thought Erin, her heart sinking into her shoes. I thought I finished that forever yesterday.

"Now—" began Mrs. Sbrocchi briskly. Then she noticed several rolls of coins that had been removed from the small safe beside the desk. She handed them to Erin.

"Mrs. Eberhardt came back here for change and she never got it," said Mrs. Sbrocchi. "Take that out to her first, please, dear."

So Erin delivered the change to the counter, where she found Mrs. Eberhardt looking grim. She was globbing mayonnaise into a batch of coleslaw in the large stainless steel mixing bowl.

"Mrs. Eberhardt . . ." said Erin hesitantly.

"Yes?" said Mrs. Eberhardt curtly. She begin to mix the coleslaw furiously with a large fork.

"I . . . uh, hope you washed that bowl," said Erin.

Mrs. Eberhardt whirled on her. She was obviously still angry from her row with Mrs. Sbrocchi and seized the chance to take it out on Erin.

"Erin, just because I'm not as good a cook as your mother doesn't mean I'm *dirty.*"

"No, I didn't mean—"

"My kitchen is as clean as anybody's!" she raged on.

"I'm sorry, but—"

"Erin, please allow me to decide the difference between a dirty bowl and a clean one."

"But—"

"I don't want to hear any more about it," said Mrs. Eberhardt, and waved Erin away.

Erin walked slowly to the back of the shop. Part of her was just as angry with Mrs. Eberhardt as Mrs. Eberhardt was angry with her. But another part of her worried about the customers who might be sharing their coleslaw with the hot, wet tongue of a dog named Loaf. Should she tell Mrs. Sbrocchi?

Well, it wasn't nice to tell on people. Any anyway, she decided, Mrs. Eberhardt hadn't really said whether she'd washed the bowl or not. So Erin sat, not very happily, beside Mrs. Sbrocchi and made a note in her head not to sneak a mouthful of coleslaw for the next couple of days, just in case.

Erin desperately tried to follow what Mrs. Sbrocchi

86

was doing as she cheerfully chattered away about mark-ups and discounts. All the while she scattered numbers all over the margins of invoices. Every now and then Mrs. Sbrocchi stabbed her fingers at a calculator, produced an answer, said "See? Wasn't that easy?" and wrote the number down on a price label.

Why do they *always* say it's easy? wondered Erin.

She tried to imitate what Mrs. Sbrocchi had done while the owner stood impatiently behind her. As usual, she got hopelessly confused. Fifteen minutes later Erin was nearly in tears and Mrs. Sbrocchi was slowly steaming.

"What are you *doing*, Erin?" she asked. "I show you an easy way. You do it a hard way that even I can't follow."

"I can't follow it either," said Erin miserably as they both stared at the price she had marked on the sticker. It was meant to go on a can of lobster, and the sticker said thirty-nine cents.

"Thirty-nine cents!" said Mrs. Sbrocchi. "The can cost me three dollars and now you want to sell it for thirty-nine cents. At least your mother *overcharged* the customers. *You* want to give the store away!"

Erin hung her head and said nothing.

After a long silence Mrs. Sbrocchi took a deep breath and got hold of her temper. She patted Erin on the shoulder.

"Let's both take a break," she said. "We'll go out and do the dishes."

The store was empty except for Mrs. Eberhardt, who was scraping coleslaw out of the stainless steel bowl into a tray in the display case.

Mrs. Sbrocchi plucked a plastic spoon from those laid out for customers, ducked under the counter, and reached under Mrs. Eberhardt's arm. She scooped up a bit of coleslaw and popped it into her mouth.

"Mmm," she said. "That's good! Now we're getting somewhere, Mrs. Eberhardt!"

Mrs. Eberhardt, whose face had been sour a moment before, now beamed with pleasure. "Goodness, that's the first time you've ever said that," she said.

Mrs. Sbrocchi squeezed her arm. "Don't worry, you'll get better. When you're as bad as you are, you can only get better."

"Well," spluttered Mrs. Eberhardt. "I don't know if that's a compliment or not." But she was still pleased, and they all laughed, including Erin, who had moved around to start filling the sink for the dishes.

Then Mrs. Sbrocchi stepped back with a slight frown and said, "I hope you washed the bowl, though."

"I, er . . ." said Mrs. Eberhardt. "It wasn't necessary. It was clean."

"Then you washed it, Erin?" said Mrs. Sbrocchi.

"No," said Erin, growing nervous.

Mrs. Sbrocchi went all silent and pale. For a horrible moment Erin thought she was going to faint. But she wasn't fainting at all. She was working herself up into a rage. "Do you realize that I fed the dog a whole pile of meat scraps and leftover meatballs in that bowl?"

"Oh," said Mrs. Eberhardt. She looked crestfallen. "Well, it looked clean."

"Was it warm?"

"Yes," said Mrs. Eberhardt. "I thought it had just been washed."

"Well, let me tell you something, Mrs. Eberhardt. It looked clean because the dog always licks it clean. And it was warm because it was sitting in the sun, breeding millions and millions of germs from the dog's tongue and the meat, which are now mixed in with the coleslaw."

"Oh," said Mrs. Eberhardt, looking miserable.

" 'Oh'? Do you know what you've done?" shouted Mrs. Sbrocchi, suddenly so loud that the other two jumped. "You've poisoned your boss! That's the kind of help I get around here! I get poisoned!"

"I tasted some too," said Mrs. Eberhardt in a small voice.

"Good!" shouted Mrs. Sbrocchi. "That makes me feel much better. We're both poisoned! And now, before we poison anyone else—" She seized the tray of coleslaw and marched to the sink. She pulled the plug on Erin's dishwater. There was a sucking gurgle as the water ran out, then the now familiar *ka-splop* as yet another of Mrs. Eberhardt's salads hit the sink on its way to the garbage disposal.

"Surely when you picked up the bowl outside the door—" raged Mrs. Sbrocchi.

"But I didn't pick it up," said Mrs. Eberhardt.

Suddenly Erin was the center of attention.

"I tried to tell—" began Erin.

"Tell? What's to tell?" shouted Mrs. Sbrocchi. "You put the bowl with the dirty dishes, right?"

Erin admitted that she had left it on the counter. "But I said . . ." she began.

"Told? Said? What does it matter? You've both poisoned me! It serves me right for hiring a child. You can't even do the dishes properly. You go back in there and work on your math where you can't do any damage."

Erin, feeling terrible, slowly started back toward the office.

"And don't put a label on anything until I've checked the price. And don't mess up Mrs. Eberhardt's invoices—oh!"

She suddenly stopped shouting and clutched her stomach.

"I feel ill," she said. "I'm going to be sick."

Erin and Mrs. Eberhardt watched her rush next door to the dress shop, which had a small bathroom.

"I'm sure it's her imagination," said Mrs. Eberhardt, looking a little white herself. "I feel fine."

Erin said nothing in reply. She was not planning ever to speak to Mrs. Eberhardt again. She had tried to tell the woman about the bowl, but no, Mrs. Eberhardt knew better. And now look where I am, thought Erin. She trudged back to the office. I can't do math. I can't even wash dishes. I'm good for nothing.

For the next two hours she sat in the office with the door closed, dripping hot tears onto the invoices and the calculator.

Mrs. Sbrocchi was only suffering from gas. She came back into the store a little while later. Erin could hear her complaining loudly every now and then through the closed door. This meant that there were no customers in the shop. She was bullying Mrs. Eberhardt without disturbing anyone.

Erin was left alone. For the life of her, she couldn't imagine why Mrs. Eberhardt didn't quit.

By lunchtime Mrs. Sbrocchi's anger had subsided. Erin was surprised by a nice thick corned beef sandwich brought to the desk.

"How're you doing?" said Mrs. Sbrocchi in a friendly way.

Erin was not as forgiving as Mrs. Sbrocchi was. She just put her head down and said nothing. Mrs. Sbrocchi reached over and picked up the sheet of price labels. Erin had so far managed to fill in only three. One of those was corrected with a black blotch.

Mrs. Sbrocchi snorted. Somewhat to Erin's surprise, though, she didn't tell Erin to stop and do something else. "Carry on" was all she said as she left the office and closed the door behind her.

Carry on? For how long? Forever? That's how long it was going to take her. In a month of bad days, this day was the worst. Perhaps the worst in her life. She could only hope that her mother got that new job and rescued her from this horrible place.

Just before four in the afternoon, Erin could stand it no longer. She mumbled an excuse to Mrs. Sbrocchi about being home before five, then fled into the afternoon sunshine. Saturday had been a disaster.

But Erin's troubles didn't end at work. She walked in her front door, and what did she hear?

"Where is everybody?" called her mother from the kitchen. Erin groaned. The perfect ending to a miserable day. Her mother had come back early. Once again Erin would have to lie.

Thankfully, she found her mother still in her coat, putting groceries into the refrigerator. Mrs. McEwan had just arrived herself.

"Where's your dad?"

Erin explained about the call from the hospital.

"Oh, the poor man!" said her mother. "He must be asleep on his feet by now."

"But listen, Mom," said Erin, "What about your job?"

"Well . . ." said her mother. She looked disappointed, and Erin's hopes fell. Then Mrs. McEwan winked and said, "I think I've got it."

"Ooo!" squealed Erin, and she leaped up and hugged

her mother. Thank heavens! she thought. I won't have to go back to that horrible Sbrocchi's.

"I only said 'think,' mind you," warned her mother. "But it's practically certain. Mr. Donat—he's the chef—says he wants me, but it has to go through the personnel office in Toronto. They're a big chain of hotels, you know," her mother added proudly.

"I can't believe it," said Erin. "A real chef!"

"I can't believe it myself," said her mother. "Anyway, I bought beef roast for dinner. We can't afford it today, but with any luck we'll be able to pay for it next week. I only hope your father can stay awake long enough to eat it."

Saturday dinner was quite jolly. Mrs. McEwan's news was uplifting enough to give Erin's tired father a boost of energy. Indeed, by the time dessert arrived things had become quite silly. Everyone marched around the kitchen singing, "Hi ho, hi ho, it's off to work we go." For the rest of the evening Erin and her mother ripped up the remains of the dog-chewed linoleum on the kitchen floor while Mr. McEwan carefully measured the room. Then Erin sat down and calculated how many tiles they would need for the new floor. She did it four times, and got four different answers. The fourth time, however, her answer was the same as her father's.

So Erin went to bed feeling pleased with herself. She had kept trying and finally got it right. That was certainly more impressive than her mother's behavior. Mrs. McEwan just laughed and refused to try at all.

"Le grand chef does not do *les petites mathématiques,"* she said with a haughty sweep of her hand.

The good mood spilled over onto Sunday morning. Erin sat down at the kitchen table and carefully spread out her homework. By the time she was finished, there was not a little white duck visible on the tabletop. She had a lot of work to do. All morning she was aware that her parents kept creeping by and looking at each other and marveling at all the homework she was doing. Every night of the week *and* Sunday? Amazing! It made Erin feel very guilty.

By one o'clock in the afternoon she was just about caught up with everything she had put off during the week. Except for math.

As math time grew closer and closer Erin grew gloomier and gloomier. What have I actually done over the past week? she thought. On the good side, I tried to help out. On the bad side, I haven't even been paid yet. And Mrs. Eberhardt hasn't been fired yet. And Mrs. Sbrocchi hasn't asked Mom to come back. And anyway, it's beginning to look as if it wasn't necessary, because Mom's going to get another job. And I can't tell anyone I was helping or I'll get in trouble. Worst of all, I've missed math homework for a week and probably made absolutely certain that I'll fail my grade. All in all, thought Erin miserably, there's a lot more bad than good that's happened.

For a long time she sat and stared at her math book,

which lay closed on the table in front of her. Should she open it? Really, after what Mr. Murdoch had said, was there any point?

Suddenly she stood up. This is ridiculous. I can't work *all* the time or I'll go crazy, she thought.

She called Sherry and invited herself over.

"If you're *really* coming," said Sherry.

"I'm *really* coming," said Erin.

It can't be helped, she thought, carefully turning her eyes away from the closed math book that was staring at her accusingly from the tabletop.

9

"Aren't you going to look at it?" whispered Sherry. It was Monday, and both she and Erin had just received back last week's math test. Erin had quickly folded hers over and stuffed it in her book bag.

"Later," said Erin. After all, why should she? It wasn't a math class. They were waiting to start English. Mr. Murdoch had forgotten to return the tests on Friday and had sent them to Erin's English classroom to be handed out. Really, it was bad enough to have to be miserable about math in math class without having to be miserable about math in English too.

Erin thought she had been perfectly right to put the test away quickly. Quick as she had been, however, she was not quick enough to miss what Mr. Murdoch had written across the top: "See me after school, please."

Up until this moment, she had been wondering whether to call Mrs. Sbrocchi at lunch to say that she had to see a teacher after school and couldn't come to work. Now that she actually *did* have to see a teacher, she began to have different ideas. Should she tell the teacher that she couldn't come because she had to work after school?

It was one of those questions with no right answer. Or at least no pleasant answer. Erin hadn't quite made up her mind when, halfway through English class, something horrible happened that made up her mind for her. Her mother appeared at the classroom door, looking pale.

"I wonder if I might collect Erin early for lunch," she said to Erin's teacher, apologizing for the interruption. Erin was shocked. Nothing like this had ever happened to her before. What on earth could be wrong?

She felt the curious and sympathetic eyes of her classmates as she left. Had there been an accident? Her father? But her mother refused to say anything until they were outside the school.

"I'm terribly sorry, Erin, but everything's gone wrong," said her mother. Her voice was actually quavering.

"Is Dad all right?" said Erin.

"Oh yes, he's fine," said her mother. "But he's been calling around this morning and he's found an oil-rig job. He's talking about flying out tomorrow."

"Why?" said Erin.

"You've got to help me talk him out of it," said her mother.

"But why is he doing it *now?*" said Erin.

And while they hurried home, Mrs. McEwan told Erin all the bad news.

"Mr. Donat from the hotel called this morning," she said. "He said he was very sorry but the head office has a new rule—they'll only hire chefs with some kind of training certificate."

"But that's not fair," said Erin. "You're a great cook."

"That may be so," said Mrs. McEwan. "But I don't have a piece of paper from some school somewhere that says I'm great. Or even good. So that's that. There was nothing he could do about it."

"Oh, Mom," said Erin, and she wrapped an arm around her mother and hugged her sympathetically.

"Unfortunately, that wasn't all," added Mrs. McEwan. "About ten minutes after Mr. Donat, the unemployment insurance people called. They're the ones that pay money to you when you're out of work."

"They're going to pay you money?" said Erin hopefully.

"Yes," said her mother. "But not for another six weeks."

"But surely if they know we're desperate they'll give us money sooner?"

Mrs. McEwan was silent for a whole block.

"Surely?" said Erin again.

Finally her mother took a deep breath and said, "I'm going to tell you something, Erin. But you must promise not to tell your father, or he'll go out on the oil rigs for sure."

"Okay," said Erin.

"I wasn't fired," said Mrs. McEwan.

"Oh," said Erin, who knew perfectly well.

"I can't explain how it happened," said Mrs. Mc-Ewan. "There was a big argument. Somehow at the end of it, I quit. I know, I know," she said, holding up her hands, "it was a big mistake, but it's been made."

Erin, of course, had nothing to say. She already knew just how her mother had lost her job. "What's that got to do with the unemployment people?" she asked finally.

Mrs. McEwan sighed. "They don't like people quitting their jobs, so they have a rule that makes quitters wait longer for their money."

Mr. McEwan was in the basement looking for suitcases. At first it seemed hopeless. He was determined to take the job he had been offered.

Finally, however, Erin and her mother convinced him to wait another week. "But I hope you both realize there may not be a job for me in a week," he warned just before Erin started back for school.

That settled things for Erin. No matter how little she made from Mrs. Sbrocchi, no matter how miserable she was working in the store, it seemed certain that her family really needed the money. She would have to go back to work at the store after school.

And in spite of her best intentions it was one of those days when everything went wrong. She didn't make it back from lunch until after the last bell, so she had to collect a late slip from the office. Then there was Sherry.

Erin bumped into her tiny friend as she pushed her way through the crowded halls moments after the bell had rung to end the school day. "Aha!" said Sherry. "I just saw Mr. Murdoch and he said to remind you—"

"Let's go," said Erin, catching Sherry by the arm and tugging her into the stream of students pouring out the front doors of the school.

"But—" protested Sherry.

"I can't see Mr. Murdoch," said Erin firmly. "There *are* more important things in life than math."

But Sherry wasn't convinced. They argued about it all the way to the library.

"You can spread your books across any table you like," said Sherry with a sniff as she sat down at an empty table. "But don't expect me to look after them. I thought we were going to do all this sneaky stuff for a couple of days, maybe. Not forever."

"At least wait to walk home with me," pleaded Erin.

"I may. And I may not," said Sherry. "And if your father comes in—"

"He won't. He's working evenings now," said Erin.

"Well, if he does, as far as I'm concerned I haven't seen you since"—Sherry glanced at the clock—"since now."

It was hardly a happy trip over to Halifax on the ferry. Erin wondered what else could possibly happen to make life more difficult.

Mrs. Eberhardt was working behind the counter when

Erin arrived. She barely nodded. Her face looked strained. Another row with Mrs. Sbrocchi? Possibly, although the owner was nowhere about. She doesn't *need* to work, thought Erin. Why does she put up with Mrs. Sbrocchi?

Erin could see a stack of dirty mixing bowls in the sink, so she slipped behind the counter, donned an apron, and began to wash them. From under a bowl, Erin pulled out a glass with a smear of perfectly dreadful bright purple lipstick on it.

Erin glanced over at Mrs. Eberhardt. No, she wore her usual light frosted pink. Erin's curiosity got the better of her, and she broke the stiff silence.

"Has Mrs. Sbrocchi started to wear *purple* lipstick?"

Mrs. Eberhardt glanced over at the glass. "No," she said. "She's started another girl working during the lunchtime rush."

"Oh," said Erin, returning to her dishwashing. So things *could* get worse. Mrs. Sbrocchi had started training someone to replace her. A real worker, not just a part-time kid. There was a note in Mrs. Eberhardt's voice that seemed to say "Ha! So there, you little brat."

And then, to Erin's complete astonishment, Mrs. Eberhardt said, "I think she's training her to replace me."

"You?" said Erin after she'd recovered. "Not you. Me!"

Mrs. Eberhardt shook her head, her mouth a tight line. "No, dear. I don't think so. Well, I mean, you're only helping out temporarily anyway. But I'm the one who's letting her down the worst."

101

She worked silently for a moment and then spoke again, more to the countertop than to Erin. "You know, after spending twenty years bringing up children, I thought the only thing I *could* do was cook. Now it turns out I can't even do that. Not properly."

Erin opened her mouth to speak and then closed it again. She had been about to reassure Mrs. Eberhardt. Of course she could do something. She could do math, and bookkeeping. But surely she must know that, thought Erin.

They continued to work silently, side by side. For the first time Erin began to seriously wonder why Mrs. Eberhardt was working in the store. Erin was used to thinking of her as a horribly superior kind of woman who looked down her nose at dumb kids. The more she thought about it, the more she realized that Mrs. Eberhardt was not superior and sure of herself at all.

For a minute Erin watched Mrs. Eberhardt working. It was pathetic, really. Her clothes were all elegant and gray under her apron. She wore a pearl necklace and pearl earrings. She was pecking at a clove of garlic with a long knife like a bird pecking at a nut. The garlic skittered about on the chopping board. and every now and then a bit flaked off. Twice while Erin watched, the garlic clove flew off onto the floor. Erin had to move over at the sink each time as Mrs. Eberhardt carefully washed off the tiny little clove. Erin knew that Mrs. Eberhardt didn't like garlic much. But still, it was going to take her all day to chop it at the rate she was going. Erin's mother would have had the entire counter buried a foot deep in chopped garlic by now, her knife moving in a blur.

Erin was suddenly swept by a wave of sympathy for Mrs. Eberhardt. After all, they were both pretty much in the same boat. Erin couldn't do math. Mrs. Eberhardt's problem was cooking. Both of them were being bullied by Mrs. Sbrocchi, and neither was enjoying it much.

All at once Erin could stand the knife poking no longer. "Excuse me, Mrs. Eberhardt," she said.

"What?" said the woman curtly.

But Erin persisted. "I wonder . . ." she began timidly. "I wonder if I could show you something."

"No, I—" began Mrs. Eberhardt. But then she stopped and her expression softened somewhat. She gave a thin little smile. "Well, yes, possibly. I haven't done so well by ignoring your advice, now have I?"

So Erin showed Mrs. Eberhardt something her mother had taught her. How to hold the knife point fixed on the counter while she minced the handle up and down across the garlic. Then Erin showed her how to sweep the garlic up with the flat of the knife and flop it down in a little pile of chunks to be minced again in the same manner.

Erin quickly chopped the clove into fine bits. Mrs. Eberhardt was delighted. Then Erin showed her how to nip the ends off another clove with the knife, then crush the clove with the flat of the knife so the skin fell away easily.

"That's very sweet of you, Erin," said Mrs. Eberhardt as she slowly began to use the same technique to chop the next clove of garlic. "Especially after what happened with the dog dish."

"That's okay," said Erin.

"I tried to say something, but you know how very difficult it is to get a word in with Mrs. Sbrocchi once she starts," said Mrs. Eberhardt. She paused and went to the cash register to serve a customer.

Erin followed her, agreeing. "But she's very nice, really," she added.

"Sometimes," said Mrs. Eberhardt as she returned to her mincing. "Other times she's a real bully."

"No, not really," said Erin.

"Yes, really," said Mrs. Eberhardt.

"Yes, really," agreed Erin, and they both laughed.

"This *is* much faster," said Mrs. Eberhardt as she began to mince a third clove of garlic. "I wish Mrs. Sbrocchi was a better teacher."

"No, she's a good teacher," said Erin, once again feeling she had to be loyal.

"She's a rotten teacher," said Mrs. Eberhardt firmly.

"No," said Erin firmly. Then she thought, This is silly.

"Yes, she's a rotten teacher," admitted Erin, and they both laughed again. So much for loyalty.

"She's a bully *and* a rotten teacher," Mrs. Eberhardt said. Then they both roared with laughter, and Erin felt better than she had for days. For a little while they worked together, side by side. Erin felt she had found a friend. Someone else as miserable and picked on as she was.

"I'm sorry about the dog dish," said Mrs. Eberhardt. "It was all my fault."

"No, I should have washed it," said Erin.

They argued for a bit about whose fault it was until Mrs. Eberhardt held up her hand and said, "Really, you know, it was Mrs. Sbrocchi's fault. Imagine, a food store feeding a dog out of a mixing bowl! The health department would have a fit."

"Who would feed a *dog* out of the same bowl you use to feed people?" agreed Erin.

"It was definitely Mrs. Sbrocchi's fault," said Mrs. Eberhardt.

"Definitely," said Erin. This thought made both of them feel much better still.

Erin dried the last few bowls and stacked them away under the cupboards. Then she stopped for a moment and watched Mrs. Eberhardt, who was actually building up quite a little pile of stacked garlic. What am I doing, wondered Erin. I'm helping the woman who took my mother's job. And laughing along with her. I've got to watch it.

The trouble was, Erin naturally liked to help out. And it was her *job* to help out, when you came right down to it. Also it was very hard to spend all day hating everybody. And Mrs. Eberhardt tried to be nice, even if she sort of overdid it most of the time by acting so genteel and ladylike.

The shop bell tinkled, and Erin looked up to see Mrs. Sbrocchi bustling into the store.

"Here she is," said Erin under her breath.

Mrs. Eberhardt looked up and said, "The bully," under her breath. They both giggled.

"Well, well, nice to see everybody in a good mood," said Mrs. Sbrocchi, who was in a good mood herself.

"Dishes finished? Excellent. Now unloading!" she said to Erin. So Erin went to help carry a month's supply of Italian food—ravioli, rigatoni, lasagna, cannelloni—from the trunk of Mrs. Sbrocchi's car. It was all wrapped in little aluminum packets with cardboard tops, gourmet meals for two. Some of it was still slightly warm, fresh from the oven of a friend of Mrs. Sbrocchi's. The friend's cooking, Erin had to admit, was almost as good as her mother's. Erin and Mrs. Sbrocchi spent some time carefully placing it all in the bottom of a freezer at the back of the store after moving everything else out of the way.

"Now," said Mrs. Sbrocchi when they were finished. "Next on Erin's schedule we have, let's see, markups and discounts?"

"Oh no," groaned Erin.

Mrs. Sbrocchi gave her a hug. "Erin, there's one very bad thing you kids all learn in school. You think if you can just hang on until the bell, the class will be finished

106

and you can walk away even if your work isn't finished. Right?"

Erin shook her head.

"Yes, I'm right," said Mrs. Sbrocchi. "Except it only works that way in school, not in real life. In real life the work is there day after day, staring you in the face, waiting and waiting, until you really *finish* it. Am I right, Mrs. Eberhardt?"

Erin looked hopefully at her recent friend.

Mrs. Eberhardt grimaced. "It's true, unfortunately, Erin," she said. Mrs. Sbrocchi looked smug.

"Mrs. Sbrocchi *is* right about *that*," added Mrs. Eberhardt. She said it in such a way that Mrs. Sbrocchi looked quickly from her face to Erin's. But there was nothing to see.

"Well, come then, Erin. We're going to have to get the hang of this soon or the sale I'm planning is never going to happen. Besides, all this teaching is costing me money."

Great, thought Erin as she followed Mrs. Sbrocchi to the back of the store. Now she's starting to complain because I'm wasting her money. That'll really help me learn faster.

They had to do some tidying first. Mrs. Sbrocchi had spent much of the morning trying to find out why she was making too much money. There were bills and invoices hanging off the desk and the shelves, draped on the floor, and spread everywhere.

"Now that's a mystery I really wish you could help me with," said Mrs. Sbrocchi as they stacked the paper into piles at the back of the desk. Erin wished she could help too. But it had to do with math. Erin knew in her heart that she would never in her life be able to help anyone with math.

Not at the rate she was learning, anyway. Because barely five minutes later the once-cheery Mrs. Sbrocchi was tearing her hair and shouting, "I can't stand it, Erin. You make it so difficult, and it's easy! Easy! Easy!"

Suddenly there was a bang behind them. They both looked around in astonishment and saw that the office door had been thrown open. Mrs. Eberhardt stood there, looking angry.

"You can't stand it, Mrs. Sbrocchi? Well, I can't stand it either. If you shout 'it's easy' one more time—"

"But it *is* easy," said Mrs. Sbrocchi angrily.

"It is *not* easy. It is *hard*," said Mrs. Eberhardt. *"Hard, hard, hard!"* Erin was stunned by Mrs. Eberhardt's words. It was the first time she could ever remember anybody except her friends say that math was anything but easy.

"It's not hard, Mrs. Eberhardt," said Mrs. Sbrocchi stubbornly. "I know—"

But Mrs. Eberhardt interrupted her. "What you know and what the world knows are two different things, Mrs. Sbrocchi. Are you a qualified accountant?"

"No, but—"

"Well, I have a Bachelor of Commerce degree from

the university *and* I passed all my exams to be an accountant, *and* I will not have you filling this poor girl's head with nonsense any longer!" She pushed her way into the room and crowded in between Mrs. Sbrocchi and the desk. "Math is hard, Mrs. Sbrocchi. To most of the rest of the world, if not to you."

Mrs. Eberhardt, where have you been all my life? thought Erin gratefully.

Mrs. Sbrocchi opened her mouth, but Mrs. Eberhardt was clearly not to be argued with on this point.

"Don't say it," said Mrs. Eberhardt, holding up her hand. "I've made up my mind. If there is going to be any more math teaching around here, I will do it, Mrs. Sbrocchi." And she began to shoo the owner toward the door. "You go on out front and keep turning the store into the garlic center of Nova Scotia. I'll handle the math."

"Well, I—" began Mrs. Sbrocchi. "Really, Mrs. Eberhardt, it is for me to say—" But Mrs. Eberhardt was already closing the door gently in her face. For a moment Mrs. Sbrocchi stood outside staring at her own office door, opening and closing her mouth. "Well!" she said indignantly.

Back inside the office, Mrs. Eberhardt moved to the desk and began to study the papers covering it. After a moment she flashed one of her nicest smiles and said, "Well, now, let's see if we can sort things out." Mrs.

Eberhardt spoke so confidently that for a moment Erin thought that somehow, in spite of everything, math might turn out to be easy after all.

But Mrs. Eberhardt almost seemed to read her thoughts. She patted Erin on the hand as she sat down in Mrs. Sbrocchi's chair and said, "Math is very difficult for some of us, Erin. But I'm sure you already know that?"

"Yes," admitted Erin. It was still nice to have somebody saying it was hard, though.

"Good," said Mrs. Eberhardt, beaming as if Erin had won first prize in a contest. "As long as we build on what we know, we can't help but be successful in the long run."

"But you don't find this math difficult, do you, Mrs. Eberhardt?" said Erin.

"No," said Mrs. Eberhardt. Erin's spirits fell a little. Of course it was ridiculous to expect that Mrs. Eberhardt, who had trained as an accountant, would find math difficult. Erin had asked her father about accountants. He had explained that accountants were trained to go into huge companies and handle all the mathematics necessary for buying and selling things and paying people salaries and paying taxes to the government and on and on.

Ridiculous to hope for even a second that such a person might find math difficult. Still, it had been nice sharing her feelings with Mrs. Eberhardt out at the front counter. She and Mrs. Eberhardt had something in

110

common, even if it *was* only being bullied by Mrs. Sbrocchi.

Mrs. Eberhardt fished around under her apron for her reading glasses, which were hanging by a cord from her neck. She put them on, picked up a sheet of paper covered with Erin's math, and began to study it.

"Run out and bring in one of those folding chairs from behind the counter," she said.

So Erin went back out front and collected a chair. She paused to sniff at the fragrance of the garlic that Mrs. Sbrocchi was cheerfully pounding into a mush.

"What is it?" said Erin, who loved the smell of garlic.

"Pesto," said Mrs. Sbrocchi. "Pass me the basil, but don't get too interested. Go back to your math. I'll call when it gets busy."

When Erin arrived back at the desk, she found that Mrs. Eberhardt had turned over the piece of paper Erin had been working on. Mrs. Eberhardt was staring at the other side, and frowning.

"What is this?" she said, and passed it to Erin.

"Gosh," said Erin, a familiar sinking feeling in her stomach as she studied the paper. "I think it's the last page of a math test. I must have just pulled it out of my bag thinking it was scrap." There were eight problems printed on the page, together with Erin's math in messy ink. There was a big red X from Mr. Murdoch's pen through each answer.

"Might I see the rest?" said Mrs. Eberhardt politely.

"I don't think there's much to see," said Erin sadly.

She pulled from her bag three more crumpled pages. At the top of the first page was the request to meet Mr. Murdoch, written in red, with the date. Mrs. Eberhardt glanced at her watch, which had a little calendar on it, but said nothing. At the bottom of the page was the mark, which Erin had carefully avoided looking at until now. It was one out of twenty-five.

Erin's mouth began to quiver, but Mrs. Eberhardt didn't notice at first. "One?" said Mrs. Eberhardt, searching through the forest of red X marks on the test. Finally she found the one tick mark that indicated a right answer.

"Look on the bright side," she said. "You got this one right, anyway." She stared at it for a moment.

"No, you didn't." she said cheerfully. "Your teacher didn't look closely at this. I'm afraid you've got two errors, one here . . . and one here. . . ." She showed Erin. "They've cancelled each other out and given you the right answer by mistake." Then Mrs. Eberhardt saw the tears glistening in Erin's eyes.

"Oh, my dear," she said, reaching over and putting her arm around Erin. "It's not the end of the world."

"It is," said Erin miserably. "Mr. Murdoch says I'm going to fail my grade. I can do everything else, but I can't do math."

"You can't do math yet," said Mrs. Eberhardt. "But you're off to a good start."

"I am?"

"Why, yes, you are," said Mrs. Eberhardt. "You know

math is hard. That isn't so simple to learn these days, especially when everyone"—she rolled her eyes out toward the store—"goes around saying it's *easy*."

"My teacher says it too," said Erin.

"Oh dear, how unfortunate," said Mrs. Eberhardt. Then, from a distance, they heard a faint cry for help. Mrs. Eberhardt glanced at her watch. "Goodness, the rush has started early this evening," she said as she stood.

"It must be your salads that are bringing them in," said Erin, wiping her eyes on her sleeve and trying to smile. To her surprise, Mrs. Eberhardt leaned over and pecked her on the cheek.

"Sweet of you to say so, Erin, but I very much doubt it."

As they walked toward the knot of customers at the front of the store Mrs. Eberhardt said, "I won't say don't worry about your math, Erin, because you should worry about it. Still, I think that since you have such a good solid foundation to build on—"

"I do?"

"Yes. You're way ahead of a lot of people because you know math is hard," said Mrs. Eberhardt loudly as they reached the counter. She looked significantly at Mrs. Sbrocchi as she spoke. "So I'm sure we can get somewhere with it if we work together," she said.

Halfway through the evening rush, Mrs. Eberhardt was ringing up an order at the cash register. She seemed to be somewhere else, staring off into the distance. Suddenly she paused and called to Erin, who was tidying cans and bottles along the shelves and dusting behind them.

"Erin—" she said, then paused, as if she was reluctant to continue. "I have a confession to make to you." Mrs. Eberhardt glanced at her customer, hoping that the person would be polite and not listen. Unfortunately the customer—a very large woman in a bright blue coat—was all ears.

"Back in the office, I told you I found math easy," said Mrs. Eberhardt. "Well, I do now, some of it. But only because I've worked hard at it."

"Really?" said Erin.

"Really. When I was your age, I didn't find math just hard, I found it impossible."

"Really?" said Erin, who was finding it all hard to believe.

"Me too," said the woman in the bright blue coat. Erin and Mrs. Eberhardt looked at her in surprise.

"I didn't let anybody know," continued Mrs. Eberhardt. "I just pretended that I followed what the teachers said, and tried to figure it out later."

"Me too," said the customer. They both looked at her again and the woman smiled at them.

"Only I was so bad that in the end I couldn't hide it any longer," said Mrs. Eberhardt. She finished ringing up the customer's order and began to put it in a bag. "So my parents had to get me a tutor."

Erin found herself stuck on one word. "Really?" she said.

"Luckily she was a good tutor," said Mrs. Eberhardt. "I still found math hard, but I slowly began to understand it."

"Oh, you *were* lucky," said the customer. "I understood *just* enough to scrape through without any extra help. But I never really understood what I was doing." She sighed as she took her bag of groceries. Then she leaned toward the counter and whispered, "I don't like to let people know it, but I'm hopeless with math now. I wish I'd taken the time to understand it all back then." Then she left.

"I'm afraid my parents can't afford to get me a tutor," said Erin.

"Oh dear," said Mrs. Eberhardt, and was silent after that.

"Oh dear" is right, thought Erin grimly.

There was always a lull for the last half hour of the day. Mrs. Sbrocchi disappeared into the back room, looking worried. There was a little alcove behind the counter with an oven, two microwaves, and a set of countertop burners. Mrs. Eberhardt went into the alcove. After a while, Erin heard the sound of the food processor. It seemed to go on a long time, and finally curiosity got the better of Erin. She went to look.

"What are you doing, Mrs. Eberhardt?" said Erin. Mrs.

Eberhardt was standing and watching something yellow froth in a blender.

"Whipping eggs," said Mrs. Eberhardt. She didn't look too certain about it.

"Whipping *eggs*?" said Erin.

"Mrs. Sbrocchi wants to start selling more desserts. So I'm baking cakes," said Mrs. Eberhardt. Then she bent close to Erin and whispered. "She's back in the office, at it again. She's convinced she's making more money than she should be, but she can't figure out why."

"Poor Mrs. Sbrocchi," said Erin. They both laughed.

Then Erin glanced at the scribblings on the piece of paper that sat on the counter.

"Egg *whites*, I think," said Erin, studying the paper carefully.

"Oh. Really? Is that what this squiggle means?"

"Well, I've never heard of whipping whole eggs before," said Erin.

Mrs. Eberhardt gave a loud sigh. "I *never* seem to get it right."

But Erin stopped her before she could dump the eggs in the sink. "You could make a nice cheese omelette with those," she said.

"Well . . ." said Mrs. Eberhardt uncertainly. "I *could* scramble them. But an omelette?"

She admitted to Erin she had never made an omelette. Erin, who was famous in her family for her excellent cheese omelettes, was pleased to show Mrs. Eberhardt how to make one. Erin fished a frying pan from the cupboard beside the oven. She heated the pan very hot, swirled a dab of butter in it, and then made two perfect omelettes one after the other in the blink of an eye.

Mrs. Eberhardt was impressed. "Except who's going to eat them?" They both eyed the steaming omelettes. Neither was hungry.

"There's Loaf," suggested Mrs. Eberhardt. They looked out the glass door. It had been another warm afternoon, and there was fat, smelly Loaf, loafing as always outside the door.

"No," said Erin. "He doesn't deserve them."

Beyond Loaf were two crewmen scraping paint on the bow of the *Bluenose II,* which was tied up right outside the door. They looked a lot more deserving than Loaf.

"What's going on? We smell like a greasy spoon!" shouted Mrs. Sbrocchi from the back office. She emerged to catch her two helpers handing out free omelettes to the grateful crewmen.

"What! You gave them *free* omelettes?" she cried, and chased the sailors to the door. They hardly had time to snatch plastic knives and forks on their way out.

"So who's wasting my food this time?" she said, looking from Erin to Mrs. Eberhardt.

"You are, Mrs. Sbrocchi," said Erin. "We couldn't read your writing." Mrs. Sbrocchi protested but did not prevail. Erin and Mrs. Eberhardt ganged up on her. It wasn't really a serious confrontation, and after a few minutes Mrs. Sbrocchi went back to her office, grumbling about people who were dumb enough to whip whole eggs.

Then Erin showed Mrs. Eberhardt how to whip egg whites.

"You've never done this either?" she asked in surprise, cracking an egg and plopping the yolk back and forth between the two eggshell halves until all the egg white had dripped into the bowl.

Mrs. Eberhardt admitted she'd never made a cake before without a cake mix. Erin shook her head in pity. When they had four whites in the bowl, Erin showed Mrs. Eberhardt how to beat them with a whisk.

You'll have to do it harder," said Erin.

"Still harder," she said after a minute.

At last she said, "Here, let me do it." Erin knew exactly what had to be done, but she wasn't an expert whipper, not compared to her mother. After a moment there was a snort beside her. Mrs. Sbrocchi had come back out. She snatched the bowl and the whisk out of Erin's hands.

The whisk positively flew, and in what seemed like only a few seconds the egg whites were fluffing up into snowy peaks.

"Hopeless," said Mrs. Sbrocchi, shaking her head. And she chased the other two out of the alcove. "Do something useful for a change," she called after them.

Erin and Mrs. Eberhardt began to clean the counter together. After a moment Mrs. Eberhardt turned to Erin and said, "You know, perhaps you and I can make a deal. You help me learn how to cook, and I'll do my best to tutor you in math."

"Gosh, Mrs. Eberhardt," said Erin, embarrassed. "It's nice of you to suggest it. But really, I don't know anything about cooking. Not compared to my mother."

"Well, compared to me you do," said Mrs. Eberhardt. "To be honest, Mrs. Sbrocchi was close to the truth when she said I'd brought my family up on TV dinners. I didn't really care about cooking until I realized how bad I was. Now I want to prove to myself I can learn. That is, if you'll help."

So Erin found herself making a pact. She felt that Mrs. Eberhardt was getting a very bad deal. Erin's mother had indeed taught her a few little tricks, but Erin hardly knew how to cook.

That evening Erin was exhausted as she traveled back across the harbor to Dartmouth. It had been a roller-coaster day, beginning with her mother dragging her out of class and her father threatening to leave nursing. But it had ended with a new friendship, and best of all a wrinkled pile of bills stuffed into Erin's bag that totaled nearly a hundred dollars. Payday had come at last!

Sherry was waiting, even though she had threatened not to be. She was grumpy. Erin gave her a big hug.

In the morning Mrs. McEwan came down to breakfast looking very puzzled.

"You know where I keep my rainy day money?" she asked.

"No," said Mr. McEwan, which was the truth.

"No," said Erin, which was a lie. She had found it one day while putting away clean laundry in her mother's dresser. Mrs. McEwan kept a little roll of bills stuffed inside a glove in the back of her top drawer.

Mrs. McEwan shook her head, bewildered. "I counted it this morning. There's nearly a hundred dollars more than I thought I had."

Erin's father snorted. "I've never known you to make that kind of mistake before," he said.

"No," she said. "I always think I have *more* than I really do."

"It's a miracle," said Erin's father, shaking his head.

"Anyway," said Mrs. McEwan cheerfully, "there's grocery money for at least a week more than I thought."

Everyone smiled, and Erin felt very pleased and proud. Nobody realized it, but she, youngest and smallest although not the shortest, was actually helping to feed her family.

10

"When I said I wanted to see you, it wasn't a request, it was a command," said Mr. Murdoch. He was leaning over Erin's desk at the start of math class.

"Oh," said Erin. She spoke innocently, but she was groaning inside. How had she possibly imagined that she could avoid meeting Mr. Murdoch? Now she felt miserable.

The trouble was that when Mr. Murdoch *really* got angry, he never looked terrifying at all. Not like he did when he was teasing kids from the lower grades. Erin would almost have preferred that. But instead, his little blue eyes went all watery and he looked like an ugly little orphan puppy with his tail squashed under your foot. Erin practically felt like bursting into tears.

Finally she could stand it no longer and looked away. Everyone else in the class had their heads down, pretending not to notice. Mr. Murdoch's special wounded stare was too much for anyone.

"Would it . . . could I . . . this afternoon instead?" stumbled Erin.

"Would it, could you, please," said Mr. Murdoch. At last he looked away, up to the numbers he had scrawled across the blackboard. Erin watched his eyes brighten as they always did when he came face to face with his great love in life—mathematics. As he walked back toward the board Mr. Murdoch did what he always did in math class—he began to chatter and bounce with enthusiasm.

And as always, after a few minutes he was bouncing far too fast for Erin to follow.

When school was over that afternoon, Erin stood in the hall in a quandary. Should she phone Mrs. Sbrocchi? she wondered. It was complicated trying to get to use the office phone. The nearest pay phone was a long way from the school. Rather than risk being late for Mr. Murdoch, she decided she was not important enough to be missed that badly at the store.

So she unloaded her homework and books on a not-very-pleased Sherry, and asked her friend to carry them for her to the library. Tiny Sherry finally staggered off with the mountain of textbooks while Erin slipped into Mr. Murdoch's class, which was almost perfectly empty. Perfectly empty would have meant without Mr. Murdoch. Unfortunately he was there.

"Sit," said Mr. Murdoch. He gave her a little smile but managed to look worried at the same time.

"I asked your homeroom teacher, Mr. er . . ." he said.

"Wall, Mr. Wall," supplied Erin.

"Yes, to have a chat with your parents, and I understand you all got together and had a talk," he said.

Erin nodded.

"I called your parents myself the night before last," he said.

Uh-oh, thought Erin.

"And I was happy to learn that you've been doing extra homework in math every night in the library," he said.

"Yes," said Erin.

"I was there the other evening. I saw Sherry, but I didn't see you."

Oh no! thought Erin. Does the whole *world* have to keep coming through the library? Caught at last! And by Mr. Murdoch, of all people.

Mercifully, Mr. Murdoch hadn't looked for her.

"I said hi to Sherry, not realizing you were around," he said. "Too bad. I might have been able to give you a hand."

Erin agreed that it was indeed too bad, all the while thanking her lucky stars.

"The trouble is, Erin," he said, "I haven't really seen any signs from you that the extra work is helping. What do you think?"

Erin was silent for a moment. Then something popped into her mind, and it was out of her mouth before she could stop it. "I discovered that *you* made a mistake marking my exam," said Erin.

"I did?" said Mr. Murdoch, looking surprised.

Erin rummaged through her bag and found the test.

"There," she said, pointing out the two mistakes he had made on her one right answer.

Mr. Murdoch burst out laughing. Erin tried to scowl, but it *was* sort of funny and she grinned instead. It was a shame she didn't get along with Mr. Murdoch, thought Erin. He wasn't too bad a person. Really, it wasn't his fault he taught math.

"Well," he said, "I'm not going to take your one mark away now."

"Thank you," said Erin.

"But there hasn't really been an improvement, has there? You see what I'm getting at?"

Erin had to admit that she did see.

"I actually called your parents to try to impress upon them how important a tutor is for you at this stage."

Erin opened her mouth to speak, but Mr. Murdoch held up his hand.

"I understand things aren't going so well for your family just at the moment," said Mr. Murdoch. He gave a sigh.

At last he stood up and pushed his hands into his pockets, and studied the messy scrawl of numbers on the board. "Mr. Wall tells me you're doing well in other subjects. When that's the case, I hate to hold anyone back," he said.

Erin agreed with him silently. She was sure that she hated the idea even more than he did.

"Do you know, I've always thought that mathematics was a kind of disease," he said. He smiled at the board, as if he had just recognized one of his favorite numbers.

"I thought that if I worked hard enough, I could infect anybody with that disease," he said. He sighed again and turned back to Erin. "I'm discovering, however, that you are remarkably resistant to infection."

Erin nodded. If mathematics *was* a disease, there was no question that she was still horribly healthy.

Mr. Murdoch sat down again. "Erin, I'm prepared to try even harder if you are. Are you?"

"Yes," said Erin.

"Good," said Mr. Murdoch. "Except, that unless I see . . . what? What do I want to see?" he mused. "I don't want to see all the year's math problems done over with the right answers. That's not what I want to see. What I want to see is some sign that you're *understanding*. Do you understand?"

"No," said Erin. "I mean, yes. I think I understand what you mean, but no, I don't really understand much math at the moment."

"I know," said Mr. Murdoch. "And unless you find some understanding somewhere, and I don't really know where it's going to come from, I really do think it will be best if we both try harder next year. In the same grade. Okay?"

Erin nodded dumbly.

"Erin," he said, leaning across the desk and speaking in a kindly way, "I'll be honest with you. I'm certain you're not going to find that understanding this year. I haven't yet taken the step, but I want you to realize that in *my* mind you'll be repeating your grade."

Erin tried to keep the tears out of her eyes.

11

Mrs. Sbrocchi was furious. Erin discovered her almost buried under an empty pile of cardboard boxes near the front of the store. Erin, along with several customers, had to push their way past the boxes to get in.

"You have a job, Erin! You can't just show up when you please!"

"I had to stay after school," said Erin.

"Then you should have called," said Mrs. Sbrocchi as she and Erin struggled to drag the boxes out the door, where they had to be ripped up and stuffed into one box. It was too windy to simply let the empty boxes lie around.

"I asked my biggest wholesaler to *please* deliver at three forty-five so that you and I could unpack the boxes and clear them away before the rush started," she complained. "I never would have started opening them if I'd known you were going to be late."

"Sorry," said Erin.

"Sorry isn't good enough. It's thoughtless."

Mrs. Sbrocchi bustled back into the store, swept up a stack of invoices, and handed them to Erin. "Right now all the new things are back on the storage shelves waiting to be priced," she said. "We're not going to sell any if they're stuck back there, so here's what I want you to do."

She asked Erin to find an item on the storage shelves, check to see if there were any of that item out on the shelves in the store, and if not, locate the item on the invoice. Mrs. Sbrocchi snatched up a napkin and scribbled on it furiously with a pencil.

"Right now I don't care whether you understand what you're doing or not," said Mrs. Sbrocchi. "I just want you to get prices on some things and put them out on the shelves. Use the calculator and this." She handed Erin the napkin. "Don't worry about what it means, just do it."

Erin looked at it, dismayed. It seemed to say something like "$x/.55$," only the ".55" had been ".45" and was scratched out. The division sign also appeared to have begun life, under Mrs. Sbrocchi's pencil, as a multiplication sign.

Mrs. Eberhardt was finishing up with a customer. She saw Erin studying the napkin with a look of panic on her face. For a moment Mrs. Eberhardt frowned. Then she put on her most gracious of smiles and swept over to the pair of them. She reached across from her side of the counter and plucked the napkin from Erin's hand.

"May I see that?" she said. She held it out in front of her, frowned again, then fished for her reading glasses under her apron. She put them on, held the paper even farther away, then pulled it right in to her nose, her frown deepening. Finally, much to Erin's and Mrs. Sbrocchi's surprise, she ripped the napkin in two with great ceremony and threw the pieces in the garbage.

"Mrs. Eberhardt!" said Mrs. Sbrocchi angrily.

Mrs. Eberhardt held up her hand. "I believe we agreed that I would handle Erin and math," she said. She slipped out from behind the counter. "If you'll hold the fort here for just a moment, Mrs. Sbrocchi, I'll get Erin off and running in the office."

Mrs. Sbrocchi was left opening and closing her mouth as Mrs. Eberhardt swept back to the office with Erin following her gratefully.

When the door was closed, Mrs. Eberhardt said, "She's in a dreadful mood again. She's *still* worried that she's making too much money. It's driving her crazy!" Mrs. Eberhardt shook her head, and they both grinned.

Then Mrs. Eberhardt got down to business. "Now, I'm going to let you in on a few more big secrets about math," she said. "The first was yesterday when I told you math was hard."

"I already knew that," said Erin, seizing a newly arrived jar from the shelf and studying it. "Plum Jam," said the label. They divided up the group of invoices and began to hunt for the words "Plum Jam," or "Plu Ja," or however it might be described.

129

"And I told you that you were off to a good start," said Mrs. Eberhardt.

"Sure," said Erin, not very convinced. "Here it is, I think. 'Plum Jam, Braintree, 325 g.' "

"Check the size," said Mrs. Eberhardt.

Erin examined the label closely. The jam was certainly made by Braintree, and after a moment she found the weight: "325 g."

"Now," said Mrs. Eberhardt, moving to the desk with the invoice. "This is the wholesale price that Sbrocchi's pays, $2.59."

"Uh-huh," said Erin. She knew that much now.

"And this is the suggested retail price that we charge for it, $3.62."

"Okay."

"Not okay," said Mrs. Eberhardt. "Mrs. Sbrocchi likes to sell it ten percent cheaper."

Erin opened her mouth, then closed it.

"The problem is, you don't really know what percent means, do you?"

"Sure I do," said Erin.

Mrs. Eberhardt waited and looked at Erin.

After a moment Erin said, "Well, maybe not exactly."

"Erin, the second big secret I'm going to tell you about math is this: Never, never go on to page two before you absolutely understand page one."

Sure, thought Erin, easy enough to say, but you look like a real dummy in class.

130

"If you follow that rule, after a while you'll stop looking dumb to the rest of the class, guaranteed," said Mrs. Eberhardt. Erin looked at Mrs. Eberhardt in surprise. It was just as if Mrs. Eberhardt knew exactly what she was thinking.

Mrs. Eberhardt saw the look on her face and laughed. "Don't forget I used to be just as dumb in class as you are."

Erin found it hard to believe.

"So tomorrow we'll go back to percents," said Mrs. Eberhardt. "Even if it's all the way back to page one in your math book. But for now, can you multiply the retail price—$3.62—by point nine?" She handed Erin the calculator.

Erin tried it and got $3.26.

"Good," said Mrs. Eberhardt, studying her answer. "Write that answer on a bunch of labels, stick them on the jam, then get some out on the shelves."

"That was easy," said Erin, completing her first label.

"Wrong!"

"That was hard," said Erin with a laugh. "But I did it anyway."

"Perfect! That's the spirit," said Mrs. Eberhardt. "When you're my age and you're an accountant—"

"Really?" said Erin. "When I'm an *accountant?*"

"Why not? Then you'll look back and say, math is hard, but I did it anyway. When you finish the jam," she added, "find something else and do the same thing."

"Multiply the retail price by point nine?"

"Exactly."

"Gosh, that doesn't seem too . . ." said Erin, and caught herself at the last moment.

"Easy," she finished.

"No, it's not," said Mrs. Eberhardt. "It's dreadfully hard, but you're up to the job. Now I've got to get back to work out front."

"What was all that stuff on the napkin you tore up?" said Erin.

"Ah," said Mrs. Eberhardt. She paused on her way out the door. "I'll give you one more really big secret of mathematics to think about while you're working."

Erin listened expectantly. She hoped that it might be one of those secrets that would somehow enable her to suddenly *understand* and so allow her to move up a grade like all her friends.

"There are two completely different kinds of people," said Mrs. Eberhardt. "There are those people who do careful math in their head and use paper as a scratch pad, for making odd little notes." She walked back to Mrs. Sbrocchi's desk and hunted around until she found one of Mrs. Sbrocchi's little bits of paper scrawled with numbers. "This is the scratch pad of a person who has the math all neatly organized in her head. She doesn't need to be neat on paper.

"You and I are the other kind of person," said Mrs. Eberhardt. She opened a notebook in which columns of figures were arranged neatly in straight rows. "We use our minds as scratch pads. That's all they're good for, unfortunately. Which means we have to organize and do all our math calculations very carefully on paper."

She held up Mrs. Sbrocchi's notes again. "People like this are lucky in one way. They can go quite far in math and never bother to do much more than make chicken tracks on paper."

"I think my teacher is that kind of person," said Erin.

"Quite possibly. This kind of person often really likes math." At that moment a shout for help came from the front of the shop. Mrs. Eberhardt looked annoyed. "When *he* looks at math calculations on paper, all he sees is a scratch pad for something that's going on mostly in his head. When *you* look at math calculations on paper, they've got to tell you everything you can possibly know."

"Which isn't much," said Erin.

"That's because people like you and me have to put more *on* the paper in the first place, to make the math clear." She turned to a clean page and neatly printed "Label price equals retail price times point nine." "Clear?"

Erin studied it for a moment. "Hard, but clear," she said.

There was a pained bellow from the front of the store.

"Erin, I must go," said Mrs. Eberhardt. But before she did, she held up the notebook page and said, "People like you and me may have to work harder to begin with, and be neater and more complete on paper. But when we do, we have a big advantage over the others."

"We do?" said Erin, taking the notebook and following Mrs. Eberhardt to the door.

"Yes. We can always understand each other and—"

"Mrs. Eberhardt, do hurry up!" called Mrs. Sbrocchi. Mrs. Eberhardt sighed and hurried out the office door.

"And?" said Erin, following Mrs. Eberhardt up to the front.

"And we can *go* further," said Mrs. Eberhardt. "Because sooner or later the math gets too difficult to do in *their* heads. It's like the tortoise and the hare. Tortoises like you and me plod right on past the speedy hares—the Mrs. Sbrocchis of the world—on our way to becoming accountants."

"We do?" said Erin, pausing in wonder as Mrs. Eberhardt slipped behind the counter.

"We do," said Mrs. Eberhardt firmly. "People like you and me go *all* the way to being accountants."

Mrs. Eberhardt's instructions were simple and clear. Jars and cans and little boxes began to move with surprising speed from the back out onto the shelves, each one neatly labeled. Every now and then Mrs. Sbrocchi would sneak up the aisles and check Erin's pricing. Erin would cringe. But each time all she heard was a little snort. No shouting. Another correct price! Erin felt quite proud of herself. Nevertheless, she didn't let herself get too cocky. Mr. Murdoch's words were still ringing in her ears. She needed to *understand* what she was doing and, to be honest, she didn't really.

Thanks to Mrs. Eberhardt and a jar of relish with a damaged lid, Erin finally understood the meaning of percent.

"I want you to divide this up into a hundred parts while I work on the books," said Mrs. Eberhardt as she arrived back in the office. She handed the jar of relish to a surprised Erin.

"What, this? How?" said Erin.

"I'll leave that to you," said Mrs. Eberhardt.

So Erin, not knowing why she was doing it, spread a newspaper on the floor and carefully dumped the relish onto it. Using the end of Mrs. Sbrocchi's favorite ruler ("Wash it off after and she'll never know," said Mrs. Eberhardt), Erin spent several minutes carefully scraping relish into a hundred gucky little piles, all more or less the same size.

"Finished," she said at last. "Sort of."

Mrs. Eberhardt turned from the desk, where she was working, and said, "Good. Now you understand percent."

"I do?" said Erin.

"Yes," said Mrs. Eberhardt. "You know that you can divide things up into a hundred parts."

"Not everything," said Erin.

"No, not everything. At least, not easily," said Mrs.

Eberhardt as she rummaged around in her purse. She pulled out a dollar bill and passed it over to Erin. "What about this?" said Mrs. Eberhardt. "Can you divide it into a hundred parts?"

"Do you really want me to?" said Erin with a laugh.

"If you can," said Mrs. Eberhardt.

So, feeling a little reckless, Erin found a pair of scissors. As Mrs. Eberhardt watched, she carefully cut the dollar into ten strips, then cut across the strips ten times to make one hundred little pieces of a dollar bill.

"Finished?" said Mrs. Eberhardt.

Erin nodded.

"Good. My turn now," said Mrs. Eberhardt. "Have you got a dollar?"

Gosh, thought Erin. What are we doing? She did have a dollar in her purse, but for a moment she wondered if she should admit it. Still, fair was fair, so Erin finally produced her own dollar.

"Now," said Mrs. Eberhardt with a crafty smile. "Watch this! No scissors up my sleeves." She flourished her arms and Erin's dollar about for a moment, then opened the top-right-hand drawer of the desk and dropped the dollar inside. Out of the desk she pulled two rolls with fifty pennies in each roll and passed them to Erin.

"There you are," said Mrs. Eberhardt. "One dollar divided into a hundred parts."

Erin felt foolish. "Gee, I'm sorry about your dollar," she said. "After the relish, I thought—"

"No problem," said Mrs. Eberhardt. "What I wanted

to show you was that when you divide a jar of relish up into a hundred parts, you ruin it. But money can be divided up into a hundred parts quite easily without wrecking it."

"Is that why we use money?" asked Erin.

"One of the reasons," Mrs. Eberhardt said.

"But what about percent?" said Erin.

"From now on, whenever you hear the word 'percent,' I want you to think to yourself '*Something*—' " She paused.

"Something—" echoed Erin.

" 'Divided into a hundred parts,' " said Mrs. Eberhardt.

"Like relish," said Erin. They turned to look at the mess on the floor.

"And money," said Mrs. Eberhardt. She picked up the calculator. "When you use numbers, it's particularly easy to divide something into a hundred parts."

She picked up an invoice and pointed to a wholesale price on it. "Thirty-nine dollars," she said. "Divide it into a hundred parts." She passed Erin the calculator.

"I just divide by a hundred?" said Erin after a moment.

Mrs. Eberhardt nodded. That was simple enough. Thirty-nine cents was the answer.

"You've just found the value of *one* of those hundred parts. And if you put all hundred of them back together again, what do you get?" said Mrs. Eberhardt.

Erin thought for a moment, then multiplied thirty-

137

nine by a hundred. "That's where we started," she said, and pointed at the price, thirty-nine dollars.

"Good, so—"

Suddenly there was a squeak and a clatter behind them. They both looked behind them, startled. Neither had heard Mrs. Sbrocchi come in. She had stepped right into the middle of the relish-covered newspaper and slipped. Mrs. Sbrocchi had only saved herself by clutching at a shelf and knocking several cans of Mexican hot peppers onto the floor.

To nobody's surprise, Mrs. Sbrocchi shouted at them.

"We were doing math," explained Mrs. Eberhardt.

"The jar was wrecked anyway," said Erin, apologizing for the relish.

"You think I care about a jar of relish at a time like this?" fumed Mrs. Sbrocchi as she hopped with one sticky foot to the chair, where Mrs. Eberhardt helped her sit. "You think I worry about *relish* when my staff is trying to kill me?"

Erin found a roll of paper towels, and while Mrs. Sbrocchi continued to grumble, knelt down to wipe the relish off her shoe.

"Erin, now, this is important," said Mrs. Eberhardt. "Of the hundred parts of relish on the newspaper, how many wound up on Mrs. Sbrocchi's shoe?"

"I see," said Mrs. Sbrocchi, waving her arms with great drama and jerking her foot so wildly that Erin had a hard time cleaning the shoe. "I'm not a boss anymore, I'm a math problem."

"I can't tell how many," said Erin, carefully wiping the last traces off the shoe. "They're all mushed together."

"Ah, but you *can* tell," said Mrs. Eberhardt, and pointed back to the newspaper.

Erin turned and looked, and both women watched her. After a moment she began to count.

"There are seventy-five glops left, more or less," she announced.

"And since there were a hundred to begin with—?" prompted Mrs. Eberhardt.

"A hundred, less seventy-five," began Erin, thinking hard. Then she remembered that she was one of those kinds of people who did math on paper.

"Excuse me," she said, pushing into the crowd by the desk to find a paper and pencil. Erin actually could subtract seventy-five from one hundred in her head, but she was determined to take Mrs. Eberhardt's ideas about math seriously. Mrs. Sbrocchi said nothing, curious to discover what on earth was going on in her storeroom.

"Twenty-five parts out of one hundred on Mrs. Sbrocchi's shoe," she said triumphantly as she finished her math.

"Twenty-five *percent* of a jar of relish on Mrs. Sbrocchi's shoe," said Mrs. Eberhardt. "Just another way of saying it."

"Ha!" said Mrs. Sbrocchi. "Is this how you're wasting your time and my money? Well, you'll just have to make

139

a little room for a minute, because I have to make a phone—"

And just as she said "phone"—just as if it had been asleep on the desk till it heard its name—the phone rang.

Mrs. Sbrocchi picked it up. "I was just going to call you," she said after a moment. Then she began to listen.

She listened for a long time. Mrs. Eberhardt worked around her, quietly tidying the books on the desk, while Erin picked up the mess of gloopy newspaper from the floor as quietly as she could and stuffed it into a plastic bag so it wouldn't leak into the garbage basket near the desk. As she did so, she noticed that Mrs. Sbrocchi was looking more and more worried.

"Yes, yes. I looked earlier, but I didn't think it was *that* important," said Mrs. Sbrocchi into the phone. Finally she said, "I'll look harder and call you back." When she hung up, she was looking more than worried. She was looking positively sick.

Both Erin and Mrs. Eberhardt looked at her anxiously. Then the sound of the bell tinkling at the front of the shop startled Mrs. Sbrocchi into action. "It turns out that I've got some important work to do back here for the rest of the afternoon," she said. "I wonder, Mrs. Eberhardt, if you would try to manage by yourself with the customers. Erin will help you, of course."

Mrs. Eberhardt was a little put out, but Erin was delighted. She had not really helped out in the store, except to give directions to the odd customer, since the day Mrs. Eberhardt cut her finger.

Out behind the counter, Erin confessed her difficulties with the scale, meat slicer, and cash register. Erin and Mrs. Eberhardt soon organized a sharing of the work, just as Erin and the friendly retired butcher, Mr. Przbylski, had. It seemed to make the customers happy. Erin was soon enjoying herself so much she almost forgot about her problems, as well as Mrs. Sbrocchi's, whatever they were. Every now and then, when there was a lull in the steady flow of customers, she wondered just what Mrs. Sbrocchi was doing in the back room.

It was after six thirty before Erin found out. Mrs. Sbrocchi was making a mess of the books Mrs. Eberhardt and Erin had closed up and cleaned up. They both went back to the office to get their coats and saw at once that the desk was a sea of paper. Mrs. Sbrocchi was making a dreadful mess.

Mrs. Eberhardt set her mouth in a thin line, said goodbye in a polite but cold voice, and left quickly. Erin knew how much she hated to have the books untidy.

There was still that strange, worried look on Mrs. Sbrocchi's face.

Erin hesitated as she was going out the office door. "Is anything wrong, Mrs. Sbrocchi?" she said.

"No, no," said Mrs. Sbrocchi. "Yes."

"I'm sorry," said Erin.

"Here, come give me a hug." said Mrs. Sbrocchi. "I need one."

So Erin went and gave short, fat Mrs. Sbrocchi a hug. Mrs. Sbrocchi sighed. "I think I liked it more when you didn't work for me. I got more hugs then."

"Is it anything I can help with?" said Erin.

"I don't think so, dear. You've already been a help."

"I have?"

"Yes," said Mrs. Sbrocchi. "By being the only person who couldn't possibly be my problem."

"It's a problem with somebody?" said Erin.

"Well . . ." said Mrs. Sbrocchi, uncertain. At last she motioned Erin back into the office. "It was my accountant who rang," she said.

"I thought Mrs. Eberhardt is your accountant," said Erin. Mrs. Sbrocchi explained that although Mrs. Eberhardt was trained to be an accountant, she was really just helping Mrs. Sbrocchi write things down in the company books.

"That's called bookkeeping," said Mrs. Sbrocchi.

"Is there still a problem with the money?" said Erin, remembering what Mrs. Sbrocchi had said a few days ago.

Mrs. Sbrocchi winced. "There may be," she said. "The accountant called because he thought business was getting bad."

"Is it?" said Erin.

"No, not at all. But he had noticed we were paying

less for our supplies. He thought maybe we weren't ordering as much because we weren't selling as much.

"The trouble is," said Mrs. Sbrocchi lifting a messy stack of invoices and dropping them to the desk, "we've been ordering just as much, if not more. So then he wanted to know if our suppliers have been charging us less. Ha! Fat chance! They always put prices up, not down."

"But aren't you pleased if you're paying less?" said Erin.

"It doesn't make sense, Erin. It's like getting the right answer on a math test, only by mistake."

Erin nodded. She understood that.

"Something's wrong, Erin. And no matter how hard I look, I can't find the answer." Then Mrs. Sbrocchi glanced up at Erin and seemed to read what Erin was thinking. "Yes, I know it looks like a mess, dear, but I have my own ways of doing math, and they've worked well for me in the past."

"What did your accountant think?" asked Erin.

"Oh, he had the perfect answer," said Mrs. Sbrocchi. "The problem of paying less money started when Mrs. Eberhardt began doing the bookkeeping. So my accountant suggested that maybe the *previous* bookkeeper was cheating the company by paying too much money to some friend outside the company."

Erin thought about this for a moment. "Wait a second," she said. "Weren't *you* the previous bookkeeper?"

Mrs. Sbrocchi laughed and gave Erin another hug.

"Exactly. Cheating myself. I'm afraid that's not the answer."

"Is that the only thing that would explain it?" asked Erin.

Mrs. Sbrocchi looked serious again. "Well," she said, "another possibility would be someone working here who was cheating me. A deliveryman arrives and says, 'Here's three boxes.' And somebody agrees there are three boxes and signs the invoice that there are three boxes, just like you've signed before. And I pay the company for three boxes."

"I don't understand," said Erin.

"I'm not finished. You see, there aren't three boxes. The deliveryman really delivers only two, but I pay for three."

"Why would anyone do that?"

"Well, whoever signed for three boxes here in the store could split the overpayment with the company that overcharged me."

"But you said it *stopped* when Mrs. Eberhardt started," said Erin. "So it couldn't be her." There was a long silence, and slowly something horrible came into Erin's mind.

"Wait a minute!" she said. "It had to be somebody working here *before*. But you can't mean my mother! My mother would never do anything like that. Not cheat you. Argue with you, maybe—"

"Come, come," said Mrs. Sbrocchi with a small smile. She beckoned to Erin. "Your turn for a hug. No, I think

I know your mother well enough for that." She gave Erin a long, comforting hug.

"To be honest, right now I feel more as though Mrs. Eberhardt is up to something," said Mrs. Sbrocchi. "She's so smooth and clever. But I can't figure out what it is, or how she's doing it. Not for the life of me." And once again in despair she lifted up a haystack of invoices and let them fall to the desk.

It was a worrying trip back on the ferry. True, there had been one glimmer of hope with math. She had a feeling, just a feeling, mind you, that she actually understood percentages. And that's what Mr. Murdoch wanted. Understanding. But as for everything else! Let's see now—she herself was lying, disobeying, and failing. Her family was likely soon to be starving, unless it split up first, what with her father going away. And now somebody at Sbrocchi's was cheating and stealing? Erin didn't want to think about it, but as the ferry slipped closer to Dartmouth the unthinkable kept creeping back into her mind. It just *couldn't* be her mother.

"Your mother was here looking for you," said Sherry in an I-told-you-so voice when Erin came puffing into the Dartmouth library.

"Oh no!" said Erin, frozen to the spot. She felt an actual pain in her stomach. How much more of this could she stand? She'd heard about stomach pains from ulcers caused by worry. Could kids get ulcers?

"I think I took care of it," said Sherry as she began to gather up her books. On their way home she explained that Erin's mother had arrived at four thirty in the afternoon.

"I was just about to say that you were in the bathroom when she sat down as if she was going to wait," explained Sherry. "So I said you'd had to stay late after school, and I wasn't sure when you were going to arrive."

"Why was she there?" said Erin anxiously.

"I'm supposed to give you the message," said Sherry. "She went to visit your aunt, and then she had a job interview on the other side of Halifax, so she may be late and there's cold meat and salad in the fridge."

"Whew," said Erin, thinking once again how lucky she had been.

"Well, don't start feeling too good," said Sherry. "She seemed sort of suspicious. And that started me thinking."

"Thinking what?"

"Suppose you get attacked or kidnapped or something? I'll be partly to blame," said Sherry.

"I won't."

"Well, you *will* get caught sooner or later. That's for sure. And then I'm going to be in real trouble too," said Sherry.

"No, not you, me," said Erin.

"Me too," said Sherry firmly. "I've been telling lies to my mother, and your father, and now *your* mother.

I've been telling everybody, even Mr. Murdoch, that we are studying here every afternoon. And are we?"

"No," admitted Erin.

"No. Of course I'm going to get into trouble. I want to stop this now."

"You can't stop now!" said Erin, stopping dead in the street. Sherry kept walking, so Erin had to catch up with her and say again, "You can't!" But she could do nothing to change Sherry's mind. When they finally parted company at the corner of Sherry's street, Erin had only been able to get Sherry to agree to talk about it further in the morning.

Erin's father wasn't home, and when her mother finally arrived she was so angry that she paced up and down the living room. Erin finally had to make her mother tea to get her to sit down. Mrs. McEwan sipped her tea, and after a few moments she calmed down enough to explain. "It was just a stupid short-order cook job in a terrible little restaurant," she said.

"But you can do that kind of cooking easily."

"Of course I can," said Mrs. McEwan. "But I really wanted to show the owner what I could do, so I brought along a few supplies and whipped up a few special things."

"Like what?" said Erin. She was starving and wasn't sure if she should hear this.

"Well, I did my crab hero with Spanish onion."

Erin groaned. She loved her mother's crab heroes. "What did he say?"

"He didn't seem all that impressed. So then I did my balloon sandwich."

"Oh no, not the balloon!" said Erin in agony. She would have died for one of her mother's balloon sandwiches, named by Mrs. Sbrocchi for what they did to the human figure. They were a kind of super-Italian hero on French bread, filled with prosciutto ham, sun-dried tomatoes, goat cheese, and pesto. "What did he say?"

"He asked me if I could do a grilled cheese. So I did the kind your father likes."

Erin was silent. Suddenly she saw where it was all heading.

"You know," continued Mrs. McEwan. "The ones I make with capocollo—the hot spiced ham—and Gorgonzola."

Erin groaned inwardly. "You made a blue-cheese grilled cheese?" Thanks to her mother's wide-ranging cooking, Erin ate just about everything and loved it. But she still had a problem with blue cheese.

"Gorgonzola is a big cut above blue cheese, my girl," said Mrs. McEwan.

"If you say so, Mom. So what did the man say?"

Mrs. McEwan shook her head angrily. "He said he'd lose all his customers if I worked for him."

Erin was expecting something like that. "Oh," she said.

" 'My customers want plain grilled cheese sandwiches, not poison,' he said."

"But you *know* how to make plain grilled cheese sandwiches," protested Erin.

"Of course I do. I just wanted to show him what was possible if he was interested. But somehow he got it into his head that I was going to drive all his customers away, and that was that," said Mrs. McEwan, shaking her head. "The stupid man."

Mr. McEwan arrived home a few minutes later and had to hear the whole story over, and sympathize. Then there was supper, and cleaning up, and what with one thing and another Mrs. McEwan didn't mention stopping by the library until she came into Erin's room to kiss her good night.

"That Sherry is a fine friend," she said.

"Why?" said Erin, being careful.

"Carrying your books to the library, opening them for you. I wish someone had done that for me when I was your age."

Erin agreed that Sherry was a fine friend.

"I hope you weren't in trouble?" said Mrs. McEwan on the way out.

"Pardon?" said Erin.

"Staying late at school."

"No, er . . . it was for, er . . . badminton."

"Badminton?" said her mother, surprised. "I didn't know you were interested in badminton."

"Neither did I, so I thought I'd check it out," said Erin, thinking as fast as she could.

"I thought it was a winter game," said her mother.

"Me too," said Erin, which was all she could think of. "Night-night."

"Good night," said her mother. Erin listened to her going down the stairs. Too good to work as a short-order cook? That was possible. But a thief and a cheat? Never.

12

Sherry would not give in.

"No!" she whispered to Erin in English, in geography, and in math.

"No!" she said a lot more loudly at recess and lunch.

At lunchtime Erin walked to the pay phone and called her mother. She explained that due to a big math project, she would be working a little later that night at the library, coming home a little later, without Sherry.

"What time will you be home?" said her mother.

"Nine," said Erin.

"Too dark—I'll come and fetch you," said her mother firmly.

"No, that won't be necessary," said Erin hastily. Eventually they settled on Erin walking home herself as long as it was still light, and in any case arriving no later than eight forty.

As soon as Erin walked in the door at Sbrocchi's she noticed a strange, tight feeling in the air. She had all but forgotten Mrs. Sbrocchi's problem. Mrs. Sbrocchi herself clearly hadn't. She was bustling about the store, at top speed. She gave Erin a quick, distracted smile and kept moving.

Erin began the dishwashing, as she always did when she arrived. There was more ghastly purple lipstick on a glass. Erin wondered how this new lunchtime helper, whom she had never seen, was doing. As she worked she glanced over at Mrs. Sbrocchi. The owner had a clipboard and was counting things on the shelves. Once or twice Erin caught Mrs. Sbrocchi looking at Mrs. Eberhardt, who was serving behind the counter. They were cold, hard looks, and they made Erin shiver. She was glad that Mrs. Sbrocchi thought that she, Erin, was the only one who couldn't possibly be stealing.

But why, then, when the weekly yogurt shipment arrived, was Erin not allowed to count it and sign for it, as she usually did? Today Mrs. Sbrocchi waved her back behind the counter with instructions to wipe out the display coolers. Mrs. Sbrocchi herself stood over the deliveryman and counted, then signed.

The change disturbed Erin. Could Mrs. Sbrocchi possibly believe that little Erin McEwan was able to shuffle money and invoices around in order to steal?

Too silly to think about, but Erin did. The more she thought about it, the more worried she became, but for a different reason. If Mrs. Sbrocchi now thought it was necessary to watch deliveries carefully, then she still must believe that some worker had been cheating by signing for incorrect deliveries. And that worker could only be Erin's mother.

Gosh, thought Erin, and her stomach gave her a little twinge of pain. What if it all gets really serious? What if the police start investigating?

At about four thirty Mrs. Sbrocchi came to the front counter and pointed out that the Greek salad and the bean salad were running low.

"I'll get right to it," said Mrs. Eberhardt.

"I'd rather do it myself," said Mrs. Sbrocchi. Mrs. Eberhardt looked hurt.

"But there's plenty to do," said Mrs. Sbrocchi. "We've simply got to get twenty percent marked off all our European canned goods." Erin felt guilty and looked at her shoes.

Mrs. Sbrocchi had been trying to organize the sale for several days, but Erin's math lessons had been holding things up. The trouble was, in less than a month tourists would be flocking through the shop. They bought different kinds of things than the local people did and Mrs. Sbrocchi had to make space on the shelves.

"No problem," said Mrs. Eberhardt with one of her best smiles. "Erin and I were on the very edge of just whizzing right through all the repricing."

"We were?" said Erin as they walked back to the office. She didn't feel quite as confident about it as Mrs. Eberhardt did.

"We were," said Mrs. Eberhardt firmly. She picked up the calculator and handed it to Erin.

"Ready?" said Mrs. Eberhardt.

"Ready," said Erin, and squeezed her eyes shut as if she was about to be hit by a bucket of cold water. They both laughed.

"Tell me, what are Mrs. Eberhardt's Famous Math Secrets?"

"Er . . ." said Erin.

"Math is hard," prompted Mrs. Eberhardt.

"I *know* that," said Erin.

"Good, and what else?"

"Don't go on to page two before you understand page one."

"And?"

"Some people do math in their head—" said Erin.

"And you do it where?"

"I'm the kind that does it on paper," Erin said, moving to the desk.

"All of it on paper," said Mrs. Eberhardt, taking a can off a shelf and bringing it over. "Every single step, every time."

She plonked a can of cocktail sausages on the desk. "Percent," said Mrs. Eberhardt. "*Something* . . . divided into a hundred parts."

"You want me to open the can and cut the sausages to bits?" said Erin.

"No, silly," said Mrs. Eberhardt. "I want you to cut the *price* into a hundred parts."

Under Mrs. Eberhardt's guidance Erin wrote on a piece

of paper, "100 parts equals"—then she glanced at the price on the can and wrote, "$4.90."

"Now, how big is *one* of those parts?" said Mrs. Eberhardt.

So Erin wrote, "1 of those 100 parts is $4.90"—she paused—"divided by *one* hundred?" she asked.

"Exactly," said Mrs. Eberhardt. So Erin completed the sentence with, "$4.90 divided by 100."

"Do you want me to do the division on the paper?"

"For that you can use the calculator."

The calculator said ".049" when it had performed the division. Erin frowned. "How much money is that?"

"Don't worry about it," said Mrs. Eberhardt. "We don't so much want to know what one part of one hundred is, as twenty parts."

Erin's frown deepened.

"Twenty percent," prompted Mrs. Eberhardt.

"Oh yes, what Mrs. Sbrocchi wants to take off the price," said Erin. She looked at the .049 on the calculator. "If this is one part . . . then twenty parts is . . ." After a moment she multiplied the .049 by twenty.

"Is point ninety-eight," she said.

"And ninety-eight parts of a dollar is?" said Mrs. Eberhardt.

"Ninety-eight cents," said Erin triumphantly. "We take ninety-eight cents off the price."

After that it was easy.

All afternoon Erin divided prices by one hundred to

find one percent. Then, writing down each step, she multiplied the result by twenty to find the twenty percent that Mrs. Sbrocchi wanted subtracted from all the goods on sale.

This is fun, thought Erin after she brought her umpteenth calculation out to the front counter to be checked. Mrs. Eberhardt looked at it, frowned for the umpteenth time, and said, "Right again. This is getting very boring, Erin."

By the time the store closed Erin had made quite a dent in the repricing of cans for the sale.

Mrs. Sbrocchi seemed pleased—as pleased as a person could look with a small frown on her face and a faraway look in her eyes. As soon as they locked the doors Mrs. Sbrocchi shut herself in the back room.

Mrs. Eberhardt watched her disappear. "She seems very strange today," she said.

"Um," said Erin, who of course could not tell Mrs. Eberhardt what she knew. She wished she could, though. The idea that Mrs. Eberhardt could be cheating Mrs. Sbrocchi seemed just about as unlikely as the idea that her mother had.

Before Mrs. Eberhardt left, Erin handed her a sheet of her calculations and made a small complaint.

"Will I have to write out every line, every time, for the rest of my life?" said Erin.

Mrs. Eberhardt smiled. "Well, at least you're getting the right answer every time. What do you think?"

Erin was silent. It was certainly nice to be right for a change.

Then Mrs. Eberhardt looked at the page more closely. After a moment she frowned. "What does this page remind you of?" she said.

Erin shrugged.

"It reminds *me* of Mrs. Sbrocchi's calculations," said Mrs. Eberhardt. "I know you're writing out every step, but you're doing it in a very messy way, as if you were just doing notes.

"Here," she said, and she turned the piece of paper over, placed it on the counter, and carefully wrote something on it. "What's this?"

Erin looked at it closely. "It sort of looks like a four," she said.

"Like a five-year-old might make," said Mrs. Eberhardt. Erin had to agree. Mrs. Eberhardt had deliberately made the number all squiggly.

"Now *you* make one."

Erin knew Mrs. Eberhardt was talking about neatness, so she made a very careful 4.

"Good," said Mrs. Eberhardt. "You think I'm going to bug you now about how important it is to do neat numbers, right?"

"Yup," said Erin.

"Well, I'm not," said Mrs. Eberhardt. "Surprise. In fact, if we look at your page"—she turned it over—"your numbers are always well formed, aren't they?"

Erin looked. Really, they were. "I suppose," she said doubtfully.

"Now," said Mrs. Eberhardt. "This is the last and greatest of all Mrs. Eberhardt's Famous Math Secrets. Mathematics is based not so much on well-formed numbers as on the well-formed spaces."

"On *what?*"

"A well-formed space. I want you to draw me a well-formed space."

Erin thought for a minute, then said, "How?"

"How many years have you been doing math?" said Mrs. Eberhardt, shaking her head. "And you still can't draw the most important math symbol of all, the well-formed space."

"Is it really that important?" said Erin, looking at her math and thinking that Mrs. Eberhardt must be exaggerating a little.

"Really," said Mrs. Eberhardt, surprising Erin by bending over and kissing her on the cheek. "You did very well today, my dear. And you'll do better as soon as you realize that numbers have to be carefully placed in rows and columns, separated by spaces that have to be made every bit as carefully as the numbers themselves. Think about it. Good night." And she let herself out.

Erin did think about it. But not right away. She had a more serious problem nagging at her mind. Partway through her work that afternoon Erin had stopped for a break and idly fingered through a stack of invoices on the desk. The dates were all different, she noticed. So were the companies that had sent the invoices. Erin had wondered just what the invoices had in common that caused Mrs. Sbrocchi to stack them together. There was only one thing that she could see in the end: they had all been signed by her mother. Was Mrs. Sbrocchi seriously investigating her mother? Erin had to find out.

She had to get her coat anyway. And maybe Mrs. Sbrocchi needed a hug. Erin certainly did. She knocked on the office door and slipped inside.

Mrs. Sbrocchi wasn't in the mood for hugs. She swiveled on the chair and glanced down over her glasses as Erin walked in. The glasses slipped off and fell into her lap. But she didn't laugh as she usually did.

"All tidied up?" she said briskly.

"Yes," said Erin.

"Good girl. See you tomorrow," said Mrs. Sbrocchi, and she turned back to where she was laboring over piles of paper.

Erin stood for a moment. "Mrs. Sbrocchi," she said finally.

"What?"

"You're not going to call the police about this money problem, are you?" said Erin.

"Not until I find out what the problem is," said Mrs. Sbrocchi. "And I'm afraid I still have no idea. Now run along, please, dear. I've got an awful lot to do."

Once again, Erin worried all the way home.

13

"Try me on a percent problem, Mr. Murdoch," pleaded Erin when he came by her desk the next day.

"We're working on dividing fractions," protested Mr. Murdoch.

"But I *understand* percents at last," said Erin. "Please!"

So Mr. Murdoch gave in and asked her to find thirty-three percent of two hundred and fifty-five.

Erin started calculating.

"What are you writing, a book?" said Mr. Murdoch after a moment.

Erin finally handed him her notebook and watched his face anxiously as he studied the problem.

Suddenly his jaw went slack. He clutched at his heart and began to stagger, grabbing at desks for support.

"Erin's got a percent problem right!" he announced to everybody. "The shock almost killed me." There were cheers and applause from the class, and Erin grinned foolishly.

When all the fuss had died down, Erin said, "Give me another. Go on, I can do it."

"I'd rather you got on with understanding how to divide fractions," said Mr. Murdoch.

"But you *did* say that if I could show you I was starting to *understand* math, then—" said Erin, but she stopped because Mr. Murdoch was wincing painfully.

"I did say that," said Mr. Murdoch. "But I don't think—" He stopped when he realized the whole class was listening to them.

"Look," he said quietly. "As it happens, I have a note here for you." He walked up to his desk and returned with a sealed envelope. "I'd like you to take this home to your parents. Then we'll all have a chance to talk about it."

Erin was devastated. Surely this couldn't be the bad news about failure? Not now! It wasn't fair, just as she was getting the hang of things! Everyone in the class was stealing glances at Erin. Sherry reached under the desk and squeezed Erin's leg sympathetically.

As Mr. Murdoch continued his prowl along the rows of desks, Erin stared numbly at the note, as if she could somehow burn away the envelope and read the paper inside. But there was no way of finding out what it said—not now. It was addressed to Mr. and Mrs. McEwan. Finally Erin slipped it into her bag. She tried to get her hopes up, but the return address in the top corner of the envelope made things seem pretty bleak. It said,

"Mrs. E. B. Henty, Principal, Queen Anne Elementary School, Dartmouth."

That afternoon Erin sat as usual on the top deck of the ferry. Summer was practically here. There were several sailboats out in the harbor, including the magnificent schooner *Bluenose II*, which was heading slowly out of the harbor with only one sail up.

In spite of all her troubles, the warm sunshine cheered Erin. Or at least she thought it was the sun. It was only as she stepped over black, smelly Loaf and entered Sbrocchi's that she realized the true source of her good feelings. She was actually looking forward to recalculating more prices for Mrs. Sbrocchi's sale! Looking forward to math? Amazing!

Erin's hopes were dashed the moment she walked into the shop. A customer pushed past her as she was half in the door, saying, "Good luck if you can get any service in there."

From behind the office door came the unmistakable sounds of an argument between Mrs. Sbrocchi and Mrs. Eberhardt.

I hope they get it over with quickly, thought Erin. She didn't want to interrupt them, but she also didn't really want to handle any customers on her own. As she was putting on an apron there was a bang at the back of the room and Mrs. Eberhardt burst out of the office, putting on her coat. Her face was bright pink and she did not look at all like her usual unflustered self.

"I'm going home," she announced as she passed Erin. "Having my cooking criticized is one thing. When she starts on about mistakes in math—well, that's the end!"

"What happened?" said Erin.

Mrs. Eberhardt seemed pleased to have an opportunity to tell Erin just what she thought of Mrs. Sbrocchi. "I don't know what's got into her," said Mrs. Eberhardt. "She sailed out here and started to shout at me for adding up a whole stack of invoices wrong."

"Did you?"

Mrs. Eberhardt shook her head in exasperation. "No, I didn't! *She* did. Hardly surprising, given the mess she's made of everything in there. She had two copies of one bill, so she was adding a number in twice."

"Oh. I'm sorry," said Erin, hoping that maybe if she apologized Mrs. Eberhardt would calm down.

But Mrs. Eberhardt didn't calm down. She swept to the shop door, then paused and turned to Erin. She lifted her finger and pointed an outstretched arm back at the office. "Let that be a lesson to you, Erin. People who think they can do math in their heads always meet a nasty end." And with this last cry ringing loudly through the shop, she went out and slammed the door.

After a moment Erin slipped out from behind the counter and went back to the office, just in case Mrs. Sbrocchi needed a hug.

She did.

"Thank you, Erin," she said. Her hands were shaking as she shuffled papers around in the horrible mess on the desk. "I made a mistake, I think."

"It seems like it," said Erin.

"I'll call her later when she calms down. I'm sure she didn't mean it when she said she's quitting. Really, now that she's started taking care of the bookkeeping I don't know how I got along without her," said Mrs. Sbrocchi, shaking her head.

"If Mrs. Eberhardt isn't responsible for that mistake with the money, then the only thing I can think of—" said Mrs. Sbrocchi. She paused as if she had suddenly realized who she was talking to. Erin's heart sank. It must have showed, because Mrs. Sbrocchi stood and caught Erin's hand and squeezed it. "Come now, we can't let this get all of us down. It's your job to stay cheerful, even if the rest of us are having a fight."

The shop bell rang as they stood there, then rang again. The warm sun had brought out many strollers, and Erin and Mrs. Sbrocchi were hard-pressed to handle all the customers. It was Erin's third chance to serve, and Mrs. Sbrocchi took a moment to show her how to ring an order in on the cash register.

So Erin actually got another opportunity to take in money and make change. She was delighted to discover that if she told the cash register how much money the customer had given her, the cash register told Erin how

164

much change she should give. That meant Erin didn't have to do math in her head, which, as everybody knows, is dangerous for those special people who do their math best on paper.

At six thirty everything was tidied up, and Mrs. Sbrocchi was slumped on a folding chair behind the counter. It was then that Erin admitted she still had an itch to do some more repricing for the sale. Would Mrs. Sbrocchi mind?

"Go ahead, dear," said Mrs. Sbrocchi. "I haven't the heart to face all of that tonight."

So Mrs. Sbrocchi stayed out in front and prepared some food. Erin marched into the back, armed herself with the calculator, and began again to seize cans from the shelf, one at a time, and to calculate the sale price.

Erin had planned to spend only half an hour but soon lost track of the time. Finally she had calculated a price for everything she could find on the storage shelves.

By now she was growing a little tired of calculating twenty percent reductions. She was itching to try her percentage skills on something else. She had pushed a whole rat's nest of invoices toward the back of the desk. Now she pulled some forward and took the first invoice off the pile. The invoice showed both a wholesale price and a retail price suggested by the manufacturer. No good for what she wanted. She dug down into the pile and found a small hand-typed bill from the lady who made different kinds of pâté for Mrs. Sbrocchi. There were only wholesale prices typed on the bill—the prices Mrs. Sbrocchi paid for the pâté.

Mrs. Eberhardt had calculated the retail price to go on the labels. Erin could see where she had inked the price for each item into the margin of the invoice.

By what percentage had the wholesale price been marked up?

Erin began with the wholesale price and divided by one hundred to calculate one percent. Was the markup fifty percent? She multiplied her answer by fifty. But when she added fifty percent to the wholesale price, the answer was higher than Mrs. Eberhardt's.

A fifty percent markup was obviously too high. So she tried calculating a forty-five percent markup. To her surprise and pleasure, her answer was exactly the same as Mrs. Eberhardt's. Feeling rather clever, she marked up several other items forty-five percent with her calculator, taking great care now to pay attention to Mrs. Eberhardt's Great Secret of the Well-Formed Space.

Erin quickly discovered that everything on this invoice had been marked up forty-five percent. Too bad Mrs. Eberhardt has already done it, she thought. Otherwise I would actually be doing useful work.

Was it a forty-five percent markup on every invoice? Erin wanted to check, but first she had to find some more paper to work on. She had robbed a notebook from her bag of all its clean pages. As she looked once more to see if she could find some blank paper in her bag, she noticed the note to her parents tucked in a corner. She shuddered and pushed it out of her mind. This was one evening she wasn't in a hurry to get home.

Erin began to look across the desk for clean paper. It seemed as if Mrs. Sbrocchi had scribbled across everything! Finally she found a piece of paper that had slipped between the back of the desk and the wall. At first she thought that it was completely covered with Mrs. Sbrocchi's scribbles. But she turned it over, and the other side was blank except for ruled blue lines. The paper had holes punched down each side, so Erin knew it was computer paper. It looked a little like an unused page from an invoice.

Since Mrs. Sbrocchi had already used it for scrap, Erin felt comfortable about using it herself. She began to carefully write across it "100% of," but that was as far as she got, because she saw there was a number on the paper, one printed by a computer printer. The ribbon in the printer had obviously been nearly out of ink, because the number was very faint. Erin held the sheet of paper under the desk lamp. There was nothing but a single number at the top of the page: $9,670.34.

That's a nice big number, thought Erin. After a moment she began to wonder what it belonged to. The more she looked at it, the more she knew it was a page from an invoice.

After a moment she began to carefully sort through the piles of invoices on the desk. They were all different shapes and sizes. Erin was looking for an invoice with the same color of printing on it, and faint numbers from a bad ribbon.

Not far down in the pile she found what she was looking for. It was an invoice from Wallace Specialty Food Imports, Halifax, Nova Scotia. Erin knew that Wallace Specialty was Mrs. Sbrocchi's largest supplier. Every month a truck arrived and left a large pile of boxes containing all of the many kinds of cans and bottles of strange tidbits that came from European countries.

There were five pages of invoice describing different items and their prices. At the very bottom of the fifth invoice Erin found a line that read, "Subtotal: $8,791.22." There was one more line after that, and it was so faint Erin had to hold it under the light. That line read, "Less 10% on orders over $5,000.00."

There was nothing else on the page. That wasn't surprising—there was no room for anything else. The final total had been pushed off onto a page all of its own— the very page that Mrs. Sbrocchi had turned into scrap paper.

"Less 10% on orders over $5,000.00," Erin read again. Well, this order was definitely more than $5,000.00. This will be fun, she thought, calculating percentages with really big numbers.

So, as she had done before with the invoices, she started off writing carefully, "100% = $8,791.22," then "1% = $8,791.22/100," then "10% = $8,791.22/100 × 10."

Erin calculated the answer and wrote it down: $879.12.

Finally she neatly wrote, "$8,791.22 - $879.12 =$," and, after using the calculator, penciled in the answer: $7,912.10.

Am I right? she wondered. She looked up at the top of the very sheet she was working on to check the faint number printed there.

It read, "$9,670.34."

Erin frowned. Darn. She had not made a mistake calculating percentages for quite a while now. Oh well, she thought to herself, I guess I'm not perfect after all. She carefully began to write out her calculations all over again with extra care.

Her next answer was exactly the same: $7,912.10. Wrong again. Erin frowned and studied the figures.

Suddenly something became very obvious. I've been taking twenty percent off prices for two days, she thought. The answer is always *less* than I started with, otherwise it wouldn't be a sale, now would it? Ten percent off also had to be less. So why on earth does the invoice say "Less 10%" and then show an answer that is *more*?

The more Erin looked at the problem, the more perplexed she became.

Finally she called in Mrs. Sbrocchi. "I've found something kind of funny," she said, and explained what she had been doing.

Mrs. Sbrocchi was just as puzzled. After a few moments she opened the little safe and took out the company checkbook.

"What was your answer?" said Mrs. Sbrocchi.

"$7,912.10," said Erin, looking at her figures. "Both times I did it."

"That's just what Mrs. Eberhardt wrote on the check," said Mrs. Sbrocchi. Erin was delighted.

"Of course Mrs. Eberhardt didn't have the last page because it was behind the desk," said Mrs. Sbrocchi, thinking hard. "So she must have done the calculation herself."

"But they asked for $9,670.34," said Erin.

"Yes, but she only *gave* them $7,912.10," said Mrs. Sbrocchi. "Which makes a difference of—"

"Wait," commanded Erin, and carefully subtracted.

"$1,758.24," she said.

"In other words, we paid them nearly two thousand dollars less than they asked for," said Mrs. Sbrocchi, who was beginning to get excited. "My accountant started all this by asking why we'd paid out roughly two thousand dollars less than we usually do over the last couple of months." She sat and thought hard for a minute. "I'm beginning to wonder—"

She stood again, opened the filing cabinet that was wedged beside the desk, and began to look through old bills and invoices.

"Here," said Mrs. Sbrocchi, pulling an invoice out of the files and plopping it down in front of Erin. "Last July." She continued to hunt through the files while Erin studied the invoice. The company name at the top was the same, Wallace Specialty Food Imports, but otherwise the invoice looked completely different. It had no holes punched down the sides, and the print on the page was crisp, unlike the little patterns of dots that Erin knew came from computer printers.

Erin turned to the last page of the invoice. The subtotal for the invoice came to a little over six thousand dollars. Below the subtotal was a line that read, "Less 10% on orders over $5,000.00." Erin quickly calculated the ten percent discount.

"This invoice is okay," she announced. "They subtracted the discount like they were supposed to."

"What about this one?" said Mrs. Sbrocchi, putting another invoice in front of Erin. It was dated the previous September and was the same kind of computer invoice as the most recent one.

"Nope," said Erin hunched over the calculator. "This one is wrong. They *added* the discount."

"And on this one. It's wrong too," she said a moment later after Mrs. Sbrocchi had handed her a November invoice.

Mrs. Sbrocchi was ecstatic. She had found all the invoices from September to the most recent in May. She quickly looked them over to confirm that Erin's calculations were right.

"Ever since they started computer billing they've been overcharging us!" she said. "Ooo, I could kiss you, Erin!" And she did.

"Not only have you cleared up the mystery of the missing money, it looks like you've earned me about ten thousand dollars that I've been sending to Wallace by

171

mistake!" She picked up one of the invoices and shook her fist at it. "I can't wait to get on the phone with these idiots."

Then she put the invoice down and said more seriously, "Of course, it's partly my fault. I never bothered to check. I just paid what they asked for.

"Oh, Erin!" she said, hugging Erin again. "You've been worth every penny I've paid you, and more. You deserve a bonus for this."

Erin thought she had never been so happy in her life. Just imagine! Solving a math problem! And not just a classroom problem, but a real one. A mystery that had stumped other, older minds.

For once nobody was moaning and groaning and holding their heads about Erin's poor math skills. Quite the opposite. Here was a real live person, right in the same room with her, who was talking about paying her extra money for, of all things, her mathematical ability! Erin let the thrill of it all go to her head. After all, it might never happen again. So she twirled out of the tiny office, giddy with pleasure. And in the dim light of the darkened store she saw the clock on the wall.

It said 8:57.

"Oh, my God," said Erin. "It's almost nine! I said I'd be home seventeen minutes ago." Erin ran back into the office, grabbed her coat, mumbled a good-bye, and bolted out into the store again.

At the front of the store she paused for a moment to button up her coat. Out of the corner of her eye she

172

suddenly noticed a pale, white glow in one of the store windows. It wasn't where she expected to see a light, so she turned to look more closely.

What she saw was the most horrible sight imaginable, worse than a monster in a nightmare. It turned her knees to water.

There, outside the store, lit by the exterior lights on the building, was the furious white face of her mother.

Even as the image burned into her mind, another shadowy figure stepped forward into the light. Then there were two pale faces. The other was the equally horrible frowning face of her father.

Slowly, unwillingly, she dragged her feet to the door. She unlocked it and took a deep breath. Then, hanging her head, she stepped out to face the music.

"How could you, Erin? How *could* you?" shouted her mother. "Deliberately disobeying us! Do you *know* you're going to fail your school grade because of this?"

Erin shook her head dumbly.

"Your principal called to change the appointment to tomorrow at noon. She said she sent us a note. What note? I go to the library looking for you, and where do I find you? *Here!*"

Erin was certain that Mrs. Sbrocchi could hear every word Mrs. McEwan was shouting but was very wisely staying hidden in the office. Mr. McEwan just stood and stared at Erin. He looked sick and betrayed. After a few more angry shouts Mrs. McEwan calmed down a little and they all started for home.

The ride back on the ferry was a nightmare. Erin tried to explain that she had only wanted to help. That only made everyone angrier. Even her father started to shout at her then, something he almost never did. "I don't need my twelve-year-old daughter running alone around two cities in the dark so I can eat!" he raged. "I can take care of this family, and I will."

Of course her father shouting made Erin cry, and she didn't remember much of the rest of the trip back except words and words beating at her through her sobbing.

14

Erin was forbidden to enter Mrs. Sbrocchi's shop ever again. She was forbidden to leave the house alone "until she was sixteen." She was still sobbing when she was sent to bed without dinner.

The next morning everyone was grim and silent. Erin was walked to school by both parents.

"Not just this morning," said her mother. "Every morning and afternoon, from now on. I can't trust you to go anywhere by yourself, not after what you've done."

Sherry came out of her street as they passed the corner and almost bumped into them. Her eyes were swollen as if she had been crying all night. She turned abruptly as she saw the McEwans and crossed over to the other side of the street to walk by herself.

"Just as well," said Erin's mother. "I don't want you hanging around with little liars like her anymore."

This made Erin feel even worse. It's not fair, she wanted to cry. Sherry was only doing what I asked her to do. Instead Erin said nothing. She knew that any words she had to say at the moment could only make things worse.

Mrs. Henty, principal of Queen Anne School, was a large, jolly woman. She laughed a great deal and was very popular with the students. Mrs. Henty was doing her best not to look cheerful, though, when the McEwans were shown into her office. Beside her sat Mr. Murdoch, looking *very* serious. The school secretary closed the door behind the McEwans, and there they were, perched on hard chairs, trapped.

Erin McEwan's Last Stand, thought Erin to herself. This Is It. The End.

"I think we all know why we're here," began Mrs. Henty, without her usual warm smile. Everyone nodded. Nobody smiled.

"I thought it was important to talk to you all about it. Erin has been stepping forward so well in so many other areas that to ask her to take a step backward now is something that takes a great deal of careful thought." Everyone nodded again.

"Now—" continued Mrs. Henty. Then she paused and looked up. Everyone's eyes followed her gaze toward the closed door. Something or someone very noisy was outside the office.

Suddenly there was a clunk and a bang against the door that made the entire roomful of people jump. The door flew open and, to everyone's open-mouthed astonishment, in burst Mrs. Sbrocchi and Mrs. Eberhardt.

176

"I'm sorry, I couldn't—" said the secretary from behind them, apologizing to the principal.

"What are *you* doing here?" said Mrs. McEwan, scowling and starting to rise until her husband put his hand on her arm.

"Am I too late?" said Mrs. Sbrocchi breathlessly.

"Excuse me, but—" began Mrs. Henty.

"A terrible mistake is being made!" cried Mrs. Sbrocchi. "This girl"—and she pointed at Erin—"is a mathematical genius!"

Her statement was so loud, and so silly, that everyone fell silent and let their jaws drop. Even Erin.

"Erin, I was asked to bring a gift for you from a very grateful company," said Mrs. Sbrocchi. She lifted forward a huge wicker basket covered in plastic wrap and stuffed with all kinds of weird and wonderful cans and jars. It had a huge red bow tied to the handle. Mrs. Sbrocchi thrust it into Erin's lap. The closest thing to her nose was a large can of expensive French snails, which Erin hated.

"If this is your way of apologizing for ruining my daughter's future—" began Mrs. McEwan, starting to rise again until Mr. McEwan stopped her.

Surprisingly, Mrs. Sbrocchi wasn't upset by this remark. "Not at all. This gift is from the *very* grateful and *very* embarrassed Wallace Specialty Food Imports," said Mrs. Sbrocchi. "They are most appreciative of the mathematical talents of Erin McEwan. It was she who spotted an error in their new computer invoicing system. An error, I might add, that my accountant could not find, that my bookkeeper, who is also an accountant, could not find"—Mrs. Sbrocchi paused to sweep her hand back at Mrs. Eberhardt, who nodded politely—"an error that *I* could not find, and that Wallace Imports had not noticed. Neither had several other businesses like mine. Erin McEwan is a mathematical genius!"

The silence in the room was complete. Everyone was staring at Erin. It made her quite embarrassed, and she found herself looking at her shoes.

Finally Mr. Murdoch said in a weak voice, "*This* Erin McEwan?

"Of course," said Mrs. Sbrocchi, and smiled at Erin through another silence.

Finally it was Erin herself who spoke up timidly. "Who's minding the store, Mrs. Sbrocchi?"

"The shop's closed, Erin. Being here was much too important. You've been a loyal employee, and I'm here to return that loyalty."

"Employee?" said Mrs. Henty, completely lost and trying to catch up.

"Why, yes, didn't you know?" said Mrs. Sbrocchi. "For the last little while Erin has been providing my company over in Halifax with excellent services, keeping us running efficiently, checking our books, and doing much of our day-to-day math." Erin winced. She thought that Mrs. Sbrocchi was overdoing it a little. Still, Erin didn't want her to stop—the praise was music to her ears.

"*This* Erin?" said Mr. Murdoch again.

"Of course," said Mrs. Sbrocchi.

Once again there was a long silence while her mother, her father, her principal, and her math teacher all stared at her in astonishment.

"I was terribly concerned that some kind of injustice was being done today," said Mrs. Sbrocchi. "So Mrs. Eberhardt and I felt that we had to come and speak up."

"Well," said Mrs. Henty. She opened her mouth and then closed it again. "On the one hand, I have—" she began, then stopped. "And on the other—" She turned and looked at Mr. Murdoch for a moment. He didn't notice. He was still dumbfounded by the news.

As for Mrs. McEwan, her face was changing colors like a chameleon, going from red to white to several shades of pink as she tried to adjust first to the invasion of the hated Mrs. Sbrocchi, then to the wonderful news about her daughter's success.

Mr. McEwan looked a little lost. He gently lifted the basket of goodies off Erin's lap and began to study the labels on the cans.

Finally Mrs. Henty cleared her throat and said, "Mr. Murdoch . . . um, I wonder if you would excuse us for just a moment."

"Who?" said Mr. Murdoch, startled. "Me?" He looked

puzzled. Then a worried look crept into his eyes. "Why, er, yes, certainly . . ." he said. He got up and went out slowly.

When he was gone and the door closed behind him, Mrs. Henty waved Mrs. Sbrocchi and Mrs. Eberhardt to chairs. Then she leaned forward and said, "I don't quite know how to put this. It's something that comes up from time to time, and frankly, Mr. Murdoch is such a pleasant, bouncy kind of person—" She smiled at the thought of pleasant, bouncy Mr. Murdoch, and the others smiled with her. "It really didn't even occur to me that, how shall I put it, Mr. Murdoch and Erin have a personality problem."

"I beg your pardon?" said Erin's mother.

"It happens from time to time, I'm afraid. Teachers are only human, and although they try their best, there are sometimes children who somehow rub them the wrong way."

"But surely Mr. Murdoch wouldn't take it out on Erin like this!" said Erin's father.

"I must say I'm surprised," said Mrs. Henty, spreading her hands in a bewildered fashion. "But you and Mr. Murdoch don't get along. Isn't that the case, dear?" She turned and looked sympathetically at Erin.

Suddenly, Erin saw a blinding light at the end of the tunnel.

She was being offered a ticket into the next grade. All she had to do was say yes.

Yes, she and Mr. Murdoch didn't get along. Put that

together with what Mrs. Sbrocchi had just announced, and with her good work in other subjects—Erin was absolutely certain if she said yes, she would go on to seventh grade.

She opened her mouth to speak. But somehow the word wouldn't come out. The trouble was, it was a lie.

There had been far too much lying just recently. Erin felt very unhappy about it. And what about Mr. Murdoch, how would he feel?

Suddenly Erin remembered what Mrs. Eberhardt had said about not going on to page two before you understood page one. What was the point in going on to seventh-grade math when she didn't understand math in sixth grade? Erin glanced over at Mrs. Eberhardt, who looked down at the floor. She knows it's a lie, thought Erin. Erin's eyes passed on to Mrs. Sbrocchi. Mrs. Sbrocchi gave her a warm beam.

But then, Mrs. Sbrocchi gave her a warm beam every time she started off on her horrible math lessons that never helped Erin at all. Erin looked back at Mrs. Eberhardt, who continued to look at the floor.

Yes or no? wondered Erin. Pass or fail?

She took a deep breath.

"No," she said.

"No?" said Mrs. Henty, her face falling. Now she was even more puzzled than before.

"But Erin—" said both her mother and Mrs. Sbrocchi together.

"Mrs. Sbrocchi, it's very nice what you said, but you know I'm not a math genius. I'm not, am I, Mrs. Eberhardt?"

"Of course you're not, Erin," said Mrs. Eberhardt. It was her turn to give Erin a warm smile now, and Erin felt better for it. "But you have been doing well lately."

Erin turned to Mrs. Henty. "I get along fine with Mr. Murdoch. Sort of," she said. "I don't understand him, but I get along with him fine."

Mrs. Henty threw up her hands. "What *is* everybody saying?" she asked.

"I'll go get Mr. Murdoch," said Erin, standing up abruptly. "He should be here." And she quickly went out of the room.

She found Mr. Murdoch sitting on the same bench that kids used when they were in trouble and waiting to see the principal. He was hunched over, but he looked less like a vulture now and more like a baby bird, one without any feathers on it.

"Erin—" he said, and his voice broke. "I'm sorry, I never thought . . . I should have realized . . . nothing like this has ever happened to me since I started teaching."

"It's okay—" Erin began, but he interrupted her.

"No, it's not okay," said Mr. Murdoch. "I can't expect everyone to like me. But it never occurred to me that you might have trouble in math because I . . . because you don't like me."

Erin sat down on the bench beside him. "Mr. Murdoch, it's okay. I like you."

"You do?" he said.

"Sort of," she said. "I mean, it's not your fault that you teach math."

He thought about that for a moment. "I guess not," he said finally.

"Somebody has to do it," said Erin.

"I guess so," he said.

"It's pretty hard, you know," she said.

"It's easy when—" he began.

Erin interrupted him. "Mr. Murdoch, I'm going to go back in there and say I really like you. So would you do me a favor?"

"What?"

"Don't say math is easy. Say, 'Math is hard, but we have to do it anyway.' "

Mr. Murdoch looked puzzled. "Will that make you feel better?"

"Yup," said Erin.

"Well," said Mr. Murdoch, standing up and holding out his hand. "It makes *me* feel better to discover you don't hate me. So what the heck, math is hard but we have to do it anyway, right?"

"Right," said Erin. And hand in hand they went back into the room.

Mrs. Sbrocchi was lecturing Mrs. McEwan. "Do you know how much money she saved me by trying a little?" said Mrs. Sbrocchi. "Ten thousand dollars! You know how much you cost me by *not* trying? I'll tell you! My business is going down the drain without your wonderful cooking."

Mrs. McEwan didn't know what to say after this outburst, so she sat there turning colors while Mr. McEwan studied the cans in the basket even harder.

"You want me to beg, don't you?" said Mrs. Sbrocchi. "All right, I'm begging. *Please* take your old job back."

"As what?" said Mrs. McEwan.

"Whatever you want," said Mrs. Sbrocchi. "All right, as assistant manager, so long as you come back."

"Since you put it that way, I suppose—" said Mrs. McEwan.

Erin did not have a fraction of a second in which to feel delighted. There was a gasp from Mrs. Eberhardt. "Well," she said in her coldest, politest tone, "I can see there's no place for me in this big happy family." She stood up and walked out.

It was all too much for Mrs. Henty, who buried her face in her hands.

Erin rushed to her mother and bent over to whisper in her ear, "Mom, you can't let her quit! It's Mrs. Eberhardt who's been helping me with my math!"

"Really?" said Mrs. McEwan, standing up. "Well, of course she can't quit then." She rushed out after Mrs. Eberhardt.

Mrs. Sbrocchi was about to follow. But she recognized a familiar note of determination in Mrs. McEwan's voice and so turned to Mr. Murdoch instead. "What do we have to do to get Erin into seventh grade?" she asked.

Mr. Murdoch was embarrassed.

"It's practice that is needed. More math practice. Am I right?" said Mrs. Sbrocchi.

"I'm afraid so," said Mr. Murdoch. "Don't you think so, Erin?"

Erin had to admit it.

"She can only get math from you?" said Mrs. Sbrocchi.

"Oh no, not at all," said Mr. Murdoch hastily "But short of a regular tutor—"

"Who's short of a regular tutor?" said Mrs. Sbrocchi. "We're not."

She turned to Erin. "Erin, I tell you what. This summer you come help me for free, all summer. Okay?"

"Okay," said Erin.

"And I'll give you Mrs. Eberhardt for enough time to get you into seventh grade, okay?"

"Okay," Erin said.

"Okay?" said Mrs. Sbrocchi turning to Mr. Murdoch.

"Well . . ." said Mr. Murdoch. This was not at all how he had expected the meeting to turn out. But something in Mrs. Sbrocchi's eye convinced him.

"Okay," he said with a grin.

"Okay?" said Mrs. Sbrocchi, turning now to Mrs. Henty.

"Why not?" said Mrs. Henty. "What do I know? I just work here." She stood and threw her arms in the air. "As far as I'm concerned, everything's okay."

"As far as we're concerned, it's not," said a voice from the door. They all turned to see Mrs. McEwan and Mrs. Eberhardt arm in arm. They were glowering at Mrs. Sbrocchi.

There was another long silence.

It was finally broken by Mr. McEwan, who had turned the gift basket around in his lap and was still studying it.

"I love snails," he said, and then looked embarrassed when everyone turned to stare at him. "I have an idea," he said. "Why don't you *all* be managers?"

And that is what they decided to do.

They all walked home to the McEwans' for tea. Not Mr. Murdoch or Mrs. Henty, who had to work, but the rest of them—including Erin, who was given the day off.

In front walked Mrs. McEwan, Mrs. Eberhardt, and Mrs. Sbrocchi, arm in arm, two short women on either side of a tall elegant one, all three chattering away.

"Of course, Margaret, now that Sally Eberhardt's with us you won't have to worry about the math," said Mrs. Sbrocchi to Mrs. McEwan.

"What do you mean? Of course I'll have to worry about it. If my daughter can do it, then so can I," said Mrs. McEwan.

"Really, it won't be necessary."

"Of course it's necessary. There's no argument," said Mrs. McEwan.

Behind walked Mr. McEwan, and that not-quite-yet math genius, soon to be in seventh grade, Erin McEwan. They smiled at each other. Why hadn't anyone thought of it before? The way to get Mrs. McEwan to learn math was so obvious: Tell her not to bother, then wait for her to disagree.

"I think we probably owe it to you that your mother got her job back," said Mr. McEwan. "I want to thank you, and say I'm sorry for shouting at you yesterday."

"I guess you had to shout," said Erin. "I'm sorry I disobeyed you and did all that lying." They walked a few blocks together in silence, happy and comfortable together for the first time in what seemed like months.

Finally Erin said, "Can I borrow a lot of money from you soon, Dad?"

"How much?"

"Fifty dollars."

"What for?"

"I think I want to buy Sherry Salisky a present. A very good one."

"Yes. I think perhaps you'd better," said her father.

Erin did borrow the money and bought a very expensive book: *An Illustrated History of Canadian Prime Ministers*. Erin could not read a single paragraph without falling asleep, but Sherry, who was planning to one day have her own chapter in the book, thought it was just about the nicest present she'd ever gotten. She forgave Erin and they became friends again.

But Erin didn't ever pay her father back, because she

didn't make any money that summer. She worked hard, though, because even though Mrs. Sbrocchi, Mrs. Eberhardt, and Mrs. McEwan (not to mention the lunchtime girl with the purple lipstick) were all working, the store was busier than ever. Mrs. Eberhardt helped Erin *and* Mrs. McEwan with math. Mrs. McEwan taught Mrs. Eberhardt how to cook.

Near the front door of the shop a little wooden sign with gold letters printed on it appeared. Under SBROCCHI'S FINE FOODS it said: MANAGER OF FOOD PREPARATION, MRS. MARGARET MCEWAN. Below that it said: MANAGER OF ADMINISTRATIVE SERVICES, MRS. SALLY EBERHARDT. Near the bottom it said: MANAGER OF MOPS AND MATHEMATICS, ERIN MCEWAN.

At the very bottom it said: OVERMANAGER, MRS. ANNA SBROCCHI, because, as Mrs. Sbrocchi said, there had never before been one store so overmanaged.

Oh yes, Erin made it into seventh grade. They had the same ugly green floor tiles in Dartmouth Junior High as they did in Queen Anne School, so Erin could stare at the floor and feel right at home. All her friends were there too. That helped.

And what about her math? She found that seventh-grade math wasn't easy either. Even when she knew how to do it.

It was *hard*.

But she did it anyway.

188